D0399221

THE MIDNIGHT BRIGADE

ADAM BORBA

ILLUSTRATIONS BY KARL KWASNY

Ⓛ Ⓑ

LITTLE, BROWN AND COMPANY

New York   Boston

Copyright © 2021 by Adam Borba

Illustrations by Karl Kwasny. Illustrations © 2021 by Adam Borba.

Cover art copyright © 2021 by Erwin Madrid. Cover design by Jenny Kimura. Cover copyright © 2021 by Hachette Book Group, Inc

Little, Brown and Company
Hachette Book Group
1290 Avenue of the Americas, New York, NY 10104

Visit us at LBYR.com

First Edition: September 2021

Little, Brown and Company is a division of Hachette Book Group, Inc. The Little, Brown name and logo are trademarks of Hachette Book Group, Inc.

The publisher is not responsible for websites (or their content) that are not owned by the publisher.

Bridge line art © grop/Shutterstock.com

Library of Congress Cataloging-in-Publication Data
Names: Borba, Adam, author.
Title: The Midnight Brigade / Adam Borba.
Description: First edition. | New York : Little, Brown and Company, 2021. | Audience: Ages 8-12. | Summary: "Three unexpected friends find a gruff yet kindhearted troll underneath their local Pittsburgh bridge who teaches them the importance of friendship and raising their voices" —Provided by publisher.
Identifiers: LCCN 2021004728 | ISBN 9730316542517 (hardcover) | ISBN 9780316542579 (ebook) | ISBN 9780316542609 (ebook other)
Subjects: CYAC: Friendship—Fiction. | Trolls—Fiction. | Pittsburgh (Pa.)—Fiction.
Classification: LCC PZ7.1.B6695 Mi 2021 | DDC [Fic]—dc23
LC record available at https://lccn.loc.gov/2021004728

ISBNs: 978-0-316-54251-7 (hardcover), 978-0-316-54257-9 (ebook)

Printed in the United States of America

LSC-C

Printing 1, 2021

For the Bold Ones,
especially Erin, Charlie, and Hazel

THE
MIDNIGHT
BRIGADE

PROLOGUE

Carl's parents were fighting again the first night it happened. Mr. and Mrs. Chesterfield fought about everything. Misunderstandings. Facts. Opinions. Neglected chores. If it was possible to squabble about something, Carl's parents did. They hadn't always been this way. But lately, Carl's father was less than happy at work, and he often brought that unhappiness home.

When his parents shouted and stomped around their bedroom, the pale-blue wall separating their room from his shook and the ancient ceiling fan above him rattled. As Carl gripped his sheets, he worried the vibrations would cause the rickety old thing to crash down on him. Why would anyone put a fan above a bed, he wondered. It seemed specifically intended to cause insomnia and nightmares.

Whenever the fighting got bad, Carl would sit on his windowsill and count bridges. There was something soothing about a sturdy bridge. He could see quite a few from his second-story perch. Thirty-three, to be exact. He took comfort in that number (though not enough comfort to stop worrying about his parents).

Then he saw it. At first he thought his parents' yelling and stomping were to blame, but he quickly decided that was impossible. A bridge wobbled. Teetered a foot to the left, then back again. Like a squirrel poking its head around a tree. Only for a moment. But bridges shouldn't move at all, at least not a bridge made from hundreds of tons of Pittsburgh steel. What could cause such a thing? He stared at the bridge until his mother yelled, "Something has to change!" Then his parents went quiet. Carl dared the bridge to budge again. Had his eyes played a trick on him? Must have, he thought as he climbed into bed. Then, as he drifted to sleep, he could've sworn he heard something deep in the city growl in pain.

———

Carl's father's side of the family had lived in Pittsburgh for five generations. Mr. Chesterfield was an engineer by trade and a bridge builder in practice. Carl thought Pittsburgh was as good a place as any for a bridge builder to live. The city had over four hundred bridges, and dozens of those had been built by Carl's father and his father before him, and Carl's great-grandfather before that. Bridge building was a noble profession, allowing Pittsburghers to travel from one end of something to the other end of something else. Without a bridge, they would be forced to go around.

Unfortunately, after a city has constructed over four hundred bridges, few places remain for new bridges to be built. So, rather than building new bridges, Carl's dad mostly repaired old ones. But bridge *repairing* wasn't what he had signed up for. Instead of designing something new, he now restored and replicated someone else's work. He missed creating. Missed making his own decisions.

Recently, the bridges in Pittsburgh needed to be repaired at a curiously high rate. Not astronomically higher than bridges elsewhere, but enough that it was noticeable to the people who kept track of that sort of thing. It troubled Carl. It also kept Mr. Chesterfield busy at work, only his heart wasn't in it. Carl's father needed to find a new noble profession. But what do Pittsburghers need as much as traveling from one end of something to the other end of something else? He pondered this aloud with his son on a Sunday stroll. It was cold for late February, but their puffy coats and Mr. Chesterfield's ability to make Carl laugh helped. Like when he rubbed his coat's sleeves against his sides to make record-scratching sounds or pretended he could only move in slow motion. As they talked, they pulled out and unwrapped two peanut butter and tomato sandwiches. And after they'd taken bites, made faces, then tossed their less-than-tasty sandwiches into the trash, something caught Mr. Chesterfield's eye.

In the trash can beneath the hardly eaten sandwiches was a newspaper with two classified ads that had been overlooked by all other Pittsburghers—two seemingly unrelated ads that would set the Chesterfield family on a life-altering path.

The first ad was for a quarter acre of land under one of Pittsburgh's oldest bridges—one that Carl's great-grandfather had helped build. The second ad was for a food truck with a busted engine and blown tires—one that had a "decently working kitchen with limited assembly required" (rust included—no extra charge). Mr. Chesterfield explained that the ads must have been placed specifically for him. And he was never wrong (except for the times when he was).

Carl did his best to unpack those thoughts as they crossed the street to a diner. He was reasonably certain two separate ads wouldn't target his father. But not wanting to rock the boat, Carl simply gave a supportive nod and listened to his dad ramble while an uneasy feeling grew inside him.

As the diner's waiter delivered plates of burgers and fries, Carl's father announced that he would buy the food truck and open it on that quarter acre of land. "What's more noble than feeding the masses?" he asked as he smacked ketchup out of a bottle and onto his plate. "It's the perfect job for me," he proclaimed.

Carl said nothing but knew his father was mistaken. Mr. Chesterfield had made the peanut butter and tomato sandwiches.

While Mr. Chesterfield boasted about how successful his soon-to-be-launched truck would be, Carl worried about the bridges his father would no longer repair. Why did they need to be repaired so often? And had that bridge outside his window actually moved?

His father sighed and explained that the damage wasn't typical wear and tear caused by Pittsburghers using the bridges to travel from one end of something to the other end of something else. The repairs needed to be done to damage that seemed intentional. And there was no way Carl had seen a bridge move—"Our bridges have been built expertly, by *Chesterfields*."

"Won't you, uh, miss working on them?" asked Carl.

"They'll be fine," said Mr. Chesterfield, scooping up his hamburger. Carl watched as his father took a chomp and continued to describe the damage, huffing with disdain "It *is* annoying, though. Chunks of steel ripped in the night, and rows and rows of deep scratches..."

It all seemed like the opposite of fine to Carl, whose stomach dropped as he watched his father chew.

"Like, um, something's taking bites out of them?" asked Carl.

"Bites? I guess that's one way to put it. It's all disrespectful, really."

"But who?" Carl wondered. Mr. Chesterfield had no answer. And to Carl's disappointment, his father didn't seem interested in finding out either. But Carl was.

That's when Carl began to suspect that Pittsburgh was secretly overrun by monsters.

CHAPTER ONE

C arl hadn't slept since the night he saw the bridge move.
Wherever he went, he had the feeling he'd just missed a
monster out of the corner of his eye. But his lack of sleep
gave him plenty of time to search for answers. He looked up the
word *monster* in the dictionary (it wasn't that useful). He checked
under his bed and in his closet. And he spent countless hours gazing out his window at the city.

Meanwhile, his father had set out to obtain a loan to start
his new business. Mr. Chesterfield didn't think borrowing money
would be an issue. As he told Carl, he had eaten three meals a day
for nearly forty years, and if that didn't qualify him to launch his
own food enterprise, what would? The twenty-one banks he visited saw things differently.

"You need relevant experience," said one bank.

"You don't even know how to cook," said another.

"You're just so incredibly average," sighed the twenty-first.

And that was all the motivation Mr. Chesterfield needed.
He was *average*. Incredibly so! He excitedly explained to his son

that if he liked something, "then by golly so will the average customer. If the banks won't give me a loan, I'll just find the money another way." Mr. Chesterfield was certain he had the instincts of the everyman, and that his food truck was bound to be a smashing success.

———————◆———————

Carl's mother disagreed. And she was the rational parent, so it was hard for Carl not to silently take her side during dinner in the family's old town house.

"You've lost your mind," said Mrs. Chesterfield.

"My plan is foolproof," said Mr. Chesterfield.

"Any plan you had would *have* to be foolproof," mumbled Mrs. Chesterfield. "How did you even convince a bank to give you a loan?"

"I took out a second mortgage instead," said Mr. Chesterfield.

Carl wasn't sure what that meant, but by the way his mother's face fell he knew that it wasn't good, so he sank into his chair.

"Are you joking?" asked Mrs. Chesterfield.

"There's no need to overreact," replied Mr. Chesterfield. "What's the big deal?"

Carl attempted to sink lower as he watched his mother's fingernails dig into the dining room table. "The big deal is that I've become accustomed to sleeping with a roof over our heads, and now you're risking our home so you can borrow money to sell food when you can barely prepare your own cereal."

Carl was used to his parents fighting, but that didn't mean he liked it. So as the argument continued, he slid all the way out of the chair and headed upstairs. As he closed the door to his room, he heard his mother shout at his father, "I can't believe you kept this a secret from me until now!"

Carl's parents were wonderful at keeping secrets. As far as he could tell, they knew little about each other beyond the obvious:

Mr. Chesterfield had wiry muscles and sun-kissed skin from decades of building things outside with his hands, and a mustache that made up for the hair he was losing on his head.

Mrs. Chesterfield wore her hair up in a perfect bun and possessed the confident chin and posture of a former ballerina.

Financially, they were in over their heads.

And they loved their son very much.

———◆———

Like most kids, Carl had a limited understanding of real estate law. Listening to his parents yell through the walls, he determined that since they had "closed escrow," they now officially owned that underdeveloped patch of land downtown. His father said it was an ideal location for his new business. His mother said his father was an idiot.

The yelling made sleep more difficult than ever. Because Carl didn't have any art or photographs on his walls to stare at, he spent the evening counting the rotations of his rickety ceiling fan in an attempt to keep his mind off the fighting.

Two hours after the argument began, it came to a sudden stop and Carl heard water running, which he knew meant his mother had taken a break to brush her teeth. Mrs. Chesterfield was a dental hygienist at the city's most respected practice for cleanings and oral surgery. She told Carl that teeth had been her passion since she was a little girl. She flossed twice a day and never had to lie about it. But lately Carl noticed that his mother had been losing her enthusiasm for teeth besides her own. He suspected that years of hearing how much patients dreaded coming for appointments had worn her down, and that she couldn't understand why others didn't love brushing as much as she did. Still, his mother continued working because there were bills to pay. He knew she wanted the best for him. Though neither of them seemed to know what that was. Meanwhile his father had secretly quit working as soon as the check from their second mortgage arrived. He presumed *he* knew best. Carl doubted that was the case.

Carl's father took a detour on the drive to school the next morning because the bridge they typically used to cross the Monongahela River was closed for repairs. "Haven't seen a shutdown of that one in my life," mumbled Mr. Chesterfield as he drummed on the steering wheel. Carl swore he saw teeth marks on the bridge as they drove past. He worried that the clues supporting a monster infestation were piling up.

A few blocks later, Mr. Chesterfield pulled in front of Carl's school. Carl thanked his father for the ride, took a deep breath, and climbed out to face the day.

Carl Chesterfield was the shortest boy in his class. He had pencil-thin arms and holes in all his jeans. His straight, dark hair was cut by his mother. He didn't have friends. His mom's awful haircuts didn't help. His shyness didn't either. Carl was a mediocre student and generally overlooked by his classmates, but he had one special skill—Carl was an excellent observer. He was the first to notice when someone got new clothes. To recognize who was out sick. To pick up on who was having a great day, or who was feeling sad. He watched. He listened. He processed. He empathized. He formed conclusions. And above all, he worried. About his parents. About strangers. About himself. But he never shared his insights or concerns with anyone. He wanted to, but what if the person he told didn't care? What then?

As an observer, he was the first (and perhaps only) student

to notice the turquoise flyer on the bulletin board cn the way to lunch:

SOMETHING IS RAVAGING
OUR BRIDGES, PEOPLE.
STAY ALERT.

CORDIALLY,
THE MB

Carl couldn't believe it. Was someone playing a joke on him? He hadn't told his theory to anyone, so how could they? Perhaps somebody actually shared his fear. He scratched his head as he wondered who The MB was. He couldn't recall having a class with anyone who had those initials. He wished he knew who had posted the flyer. Maybe that person could be a friend.

As usual, Carl was among the first students in the cafeteria, a room that always smelled of sloppy joes and all-purpose cleaner. It had been months since sloppy joes were even on the menu. Carl was never slowed by conversation or his way to lunch. Sometimes kids would snicker at his hair in the hall, but that was typically the extent of his social interaction. Mostly Carl felt invisible, which made him feel more safe than sad. Though today was different. Today, when he saw Teddy—the skinny, pale kid with all the freckles and floppy red hair, who always wore the same orange windbreaker—Teddy brought a finger to his lips and shushed him. Teddy was weird.

Carl always sat at the cafeteria's center table with open seats on either side of him, and open they would remain. Students would often eat across from Carl, but that wasn't the same as sitting with him. They'd talk to friends on their left or on their right—just never on the other side of the table, to Carl. The lunchroom, however, was a great place for Carl to observe. He was so caught up in observation that he didn't register the girl with the backward baseball cap slipping into a seat next to him. He'd seen the girl before but never noticed her, which is a distinction both small and enormous.

"Hey, Quiet Kid," she whispered. "Hold this for me."

Carl looked down to see a green metallic marker in a fist under the table. Without hesitating, he took the marker and slipped it into a pocket in his jeans. Then he looked up to see the smirk on her face. He locked eyes with the girl long enough to notice that hers were hazel.

"Thanks, Quiet Kid."

And with that she slipped away, leaving Carl to wonder.

There was a commotion outside the cafeteria after lunch. An ocean of students packed the hall. Carl pushed his way through the crowd, anxious to observe.

Principal Wilkinson was a stout man in his late fifties with a red face. This afternoon his face was redder than usual. Clearly he took issue with *Principal Wilkinson is a creep* scrawled across the not-quite-yellow eighth-grade lockers in metallic green. And perhaps he took more issue with the doodle of him below the insult. Though it was skillfully drawn, the doodle's artist had been less than flattering with Wilkinson's face.

"It wasn't me," said the girl with the backward baseball cap.

"Then who?" Principal Wilkinson asked. His pointer finger inches from her face, beads of sweat forming on his brow.

She pulled her pants pockets inside out. "Someone else who thinks you're a creep, I guess?"

The crowd gasped as Principal Wilkinson's face went from red to scarlet. He shook his head, patted a hand on the back of his neck.

"Back to class. Everyone."

The girl in the baseball cap and the rest of the crowd turned on their heels and made their ways from the lockers. Carl stood a moment longer. He'd never seen a man's head explode and feared this might be his only opportunity. You could hear a pin drop in the hallway. So of course Principal Wilkinson heard that green metallic marker hit the linoleum after it fell through a hole in the pocket of Carl's jeans.

Carl's invisibility had worn off.

On the surface, Principal Wilkinson's office was underwhelming. As a shy boy who kept to himself, Carl had never had the opportunity to be called to a principal's office. He'd always imagined it as more of a police interrogation room. Two-way mirror. A steel table with handcuffs in the middle. A no-nonsense older detective in the corner who doesn't "have time for it anymore." But this was just a cramped room with the same wooden desk his teachers had—only this desk had a very angry principal on the opposite side of it, and that very angry principal made the room much scarier than it would have been otherwise.

"I've never been so disrespected in my life," said the principal. "And you damaged school property. What do you have to say for yourself?"

Carl wondered if the principal could hear his heart pounding. He gulped and stared at Wilkinson for some time before he realized the man wouldn't speak again until he replied. It had been a while since Carl had said *anything* for himself to anyone other than his parents. He was somewhat out of his depth. And the room seemed to be spinning, which was unhelpful.

"I'm, um, sorry?"

"So, you admit it?"

"I do."

The words surprised Carl more than they did the principal. It was at that moment that Carl realized he had a crush on the girl with the backward baseball cap. And it was a moment later that Principal Wilkinson suspended Carl from school for the next two weeks.

CHAPTER TWO

After some serious soul-searching, Carl's parents came to grips with his suspension. They reasoned that it was a one-time slip, and Carl reasoned that the two of them had bigger fish to fry.

As punishment (and to fill his newly found free time), Carl spent school hours helping his father get the food truck ready. But "helping get the food truck ready" mostly consisted of Carl sitting on an empty paint bucket, working on math homework, and worrying about monsters while Mr. Chesterfield boasted about how successful his business would be.

The new truck had been towed to the quarter acre of land under a bridge. The land wasn't much to look at—mostly dirt, uneven grass, stones, and weeds. The food truck (which wasn't much to look at either) sat in front of a large pile of rocks that were stacked two school buses high. The ad hadn't mentioned the pile, but Mr. Chesterfield told Carl it was probably the reason the land was so expensive.

"The rocks will be a conversation piece for diners," Mr. Chesterfield said. "And you can't put a price on that."

Carl forced a smile.

A dozen yards from the truck were three wooden picnic tables that Carl and his father had dragged in for customers. They were covered in splinters when Mr. Chesterfield first bought them, but an afternoon of sanding made them comfortable enough for short periods of sitting.

The truck itself was caked in dirt and rust. And it was undrivable (as advertised). But it did have a decently working kitchen. Unfortunately, *decently working* and *completely working* aren't the same thing. The water didn't run. The gas didn't flow. And there were no power outlets to speak of. So there were plenty of unforeseen expenses.

Carl looked up at the bridge from his bucket and wondered if it was the one he'd seen shaking outside his bedroom window. "Do you, um, think it's safe?"

Mr. Chesterfield chuckled. "Of course!" He beamed at the bridge with pride. "You know, this one was built by your great-grandfather, and now we own a piece of land beneath it. There's something poetic about that. Maybe someday I'll write a haiku."

The boy gave his dad a supportive nod.

After further examination, Carl deemed the bridge a fine one, or at least one of Pittsburgh's four hundred best. It was a suspension bridge made of proud Pittsburgh steel with two strong towers standing tall from the ground. One tower next to his family's quarter acre and the other tower on the other side of something else. The Ohio River (which, oddly, was in Pennsylvania) flowed between. An asphalt road was suspended across the bridge (hence the name *suspension*). A series of steel cables tied the road to the towers, with each cable doing its part to hold the load. Carl thought it was an engineering marvel. He was also reasonably certain there were new scratches on its underside—ten gashes, each about a hand's length apart and as long as one of his legs.

Carl and his father scrubbed the truck to discover cream-colored paint underneath. As Carl sat back on his bucket to catch his breath, it occurred to him that the truck was kind of like a blank canvas with endless possibilities for design. As Carl began to share a few ideas for the food truck, his father politely stopped him and clarified how wrong that instinct was.

"It's like I told your mother," explained Mr. Chesterfield as he juggled cans of car wax, "the whole genius of my plan is that I alone make the decisions."

"Oh."

So Carl kept the bucket warm. Quietly cringing and keeping his opinions to himself.

The cream-colored paint was replaced with an eggshell white. Cleanly executed.

The picnic tables were painted tan to complement the truck. Conservatively done.

The menu would have things like chicken-fried steaks, turkey sandwiches, and garden salads. Thoughtfully chosen.

As Carl sat on his bucket watching it come together, he couldn't help but think the truck and its surroundings still felt like a blank canvas. He debated saying something but didn't want to upset his father. What if he hurt his feelings? What if he made a bad suggestion? And his father had been clear that he didn't want anyone else's opinions anyway.

When they finished the exterior of the food truck, Mr. Chesterfield couldn't have been more pleased. Now they just needed to remodel the kitchen. In less than a week they would open for business and their smashing successfulness could commence.

After Mrs. Chesterfield brought over dinner, Mr. Chesterfield walked her and Carl to the rock pile to marvel at the averageness of the food truck. Mr. Chesterfield beamed. Carl frowned. This was his father's food truck. Their *family's* food truck. It seemed like something he should feel connected to, something to take pride in. But he didn't, and he felt guilty about that.

Then the boy noticed his mother scowling, which oddly made him feel better. He felt connected to *her*. He watched as his mother's frown curled into a smirk, like she realized what was missing. He could tell his parents would fight that evening but also that she had a plan. One she would keep secret.

———◆———

That night Carl had a lot running through his head. And since he wouldn't dare say most of it out loud, the only way he could get it out was to write it down. So he climbed the steps to his room and pulled out the tattered journal he kept under his mattress and scribbled as fast as he could. Hopes, dreams, fears, and random musings. Most of it read like gibberish when he circled back, but the first two lines he wrote that night made him grin as he reread them before tucking the journal away and going to bed:

There once was a girl who got me suspended.
It happened while our finances were being upended.

———◆———

On Tuesday morning, Mr. Chesterfield propped his hands on his hips as he shook his head at an unshaven deliveryman next to his food truck.

"But I didn't order anything!" exclaimed Mr. Chesterfield.

The deliveryman looked at his clipboard for the eleventh time.

"You're Mr. Chesterfield?"

"Yes, but that's not the point!"

Carl sat on the paint bucket thinking the deliveryman couldn't possibly say it again.

"I have a sign for you," announced the man. Carl shook his head in disbelief.

"How many times do I have to tell you? I didn't order a sign!" yelled Mr. Chesterfield.

"Maybe I'll just leave the sign there," said the man, pointing. A twelve-foot-by-three-foot cardboard box leaned against the food truck's bumper.

"But I didn't order it!"

"Don't worry. It's paid for and everything," the deliveryman said as he headed away from the bridge. "Enjoy your sign."

"But I don't want it!"

Mr. Chesterfield's hands slipped from his hips in defeat. Carl knew his father hadn't ordered a sign. Knew he hated that cardboard box and everything it stood for. His dad hadn't selected whatever was inside.

It wasn't that Mr. Chesterfield had forgotten to order a sign. It was all very intentional, he explained. All the fancy restaurants and food trucks in town had names and signs. He would set his average enterprise apart by not having either. Carl convinced himself that this made sense as long as he didn't think about it.

Carl watched his father glare at the cardboard box like he was attempting to will it away with his mind.

"Maybe we should open it," offered Carl as he approached from his paint bucket.

Mr. Chesterfield's eyes went wide and his shoulders up. Seemingly, the idea hadn't occurred to him. He ripped open the box to find a giant purple neon sign with the word *Chesterfields's* in cursive. Carl watched his father stare at the sign for a long time, worried that he would erupt.

Finally, Mr. Chesterfield put a hand on Carl's shoulder. "I have to admit," he said. "There's something to the name. Something that feels very me."

———◆———

That afternoon Mr. Chesterfield and an electrician hoisted the oversized neon sign on top of the truck. The sign would be the first thing people saw as they approached Chesterfields's. Potential customers would know they had arrived. Mr. Chesterfield gave Carl the honor of plugging the sign into one of the truck's

newly installed outlets. Mrs. Chesterfield gasped and put a supportive hand on the boy's shoulder as it sparked on with a whir. A bright hue flooded the underside of the bridge, making everything and everyone more than a little purple.

"They were having a sale," explained Mrs. Chesterfield.

The sign produced a gentle buzz. And then the light clicked off. The family looked toward the plug.

"I think—"

And just like that the sign whirred back to life. The underside of the bridge glowed purple again.

"Odd. Maybe—"

Buzz. Click. Off.

Then right back on with a whir.

"The truck isn't wired that well. Can't really handle a sign that size," called the electrician as he slunk away from the bridge.

"We'll save some money and leave the wiring as is," said Mr. Chesterfield, shrugging.

Buzz. Click.

Mr. Chesterfield and Mrs. Chesterfield stared each other down, a fight brewing.

Carl decided it was time to give his parents some space. And perhaps just as important, find some edible food. So, as the purple light whirred, illuminating the picnic tables again, he went for a walk.

———————

Sixteen minutes later, Carl had half a hot dog in his hand and half in his belly. He felt better already. And better still as he passed a billboard of a toothy family holding an excessive number of balloons. The board advertised the upcoming City Celebration, which was a little more than a month away. SATURDAY, APRIL 27TH—DON'T MISS IT!

City Celebration was Carl's favorite day of the year. The annual all-city event honored all things Pittsburgh, not the least being its mouthwatering food. It kicked off with a parade (always with a different route, to highlight a different section of the city) and ended with a massive block party. The billboard boasted that this year's parade would be led by the Pittsburgh (Reserve) National Guard.

As Carl daydreamed of the event while waiting for a traffic light to change, he heard the most beautiful singing. Sitting under a red awning was the girl with the backward baseball cap. She was doodling on a sketchpad, headphones on and singing along to whatever it was she was listening to. He couldn't tell if it was an old song or a new one, but whatever it was, he had a hunch she made it her own.

She looked up as the song finished and saw him looking at her, then realized she had been singing aloud. The girl didn't blush. She held his gaze long enough to notice that his eyes were bluish green.

"A plain hot dog in Pittsburgh? That's almost a sin."

Carl glanced down at the half-eaten dog between the half-eaten bun.

"This city's known for bridges, steel, and hot dog garnishes," she continued. "And it just tastes better with mustard. Toppings make everything better. It's practically like you're having plain toast."

Carl continued to examine his hot dog, which had quickly become the most interesting hot dog he had ever seen.

"You *do* know how to make toast, right?"

"I've, uh, never actually been to culinary school."

She smiled.

"Thanks for not ratting me out to the principal, Quiet Kid."

He knew he needed to say something back, so he took a deep breath and said, "I'm Carl."

"He didn't happen to give the marker back to you, did he, Carl? It was my lucky one."

"No."

"Figured."

"Why'd you, um, want me to hold it?"

"I always trust my instincts. Guess I was mostly right this time."

Carl stared at his shoes to draw courage (though he wasn't sure the shoes were a help).

"Did you, uh, write that on the lockers?" he asked.

She shrugged. "Public service announcement."

"But why?"

"He went on a date with my mom."

It had never occurred to Carl that a principal would date anyone, let alone a mother. It was off-putting. Creep-ish, even. Carl wasn't sure what to say, so he stood with his mouth slightly open.

"Thanks again, Carl. One sec."

Carl watched as she ripped the sketch from her book and began writing on the back. When she finished, she folded the paper in half, handed it over, and walked off. Carl stared at that folded piece of paper. Bewildered. Like he'd never seen a folded piece of paper before.

Then, remembering how folds work, he pulled the paper's ends apart to find she had written the following:

TOAST

1) Grab some bread. Presliced is easiest for this recipe.
   If it's not presliced, please see step 1A.
1A) Slice bread.
2) Put bread in the bread slots of the toaster.
3) Choose the desired darkness setting on the toaster.
   The middle setting is usually a safe bet.
4) Push the toaster plunger down to start (make sure the toaster is plugged in—easy mistake).
5) When it pops up, carefully remove toast from toaster and set on a plate. Add parsley to plate if desired.
6) Spread butter and/or jam. (Important.)

Then he flipped the paper over. On the back was a drawing of a giant sea monster rising from a river and taking a bite out of a bridge. The creature had the body of an octopus and the head of a man who looked vaguely like Principal Wilkinson. Carl forgot to breathe for a moment. He looked up after the girl. She was gone.

CHAPTER THREE

T he food truck opened the following evening. Carl spent most of the night inside the kitchen, thinking about the girl with the backward baseball cap. He dreamed about that cap. He figured it was the greatest backward baseball cap he'd ever seen. Before long he was wondering if the girl was thinking about him while he was thinking about her (she probably wasn't).

Then he remembered her sketch of the sea monster and began to worry about the gashes underneath the bridge. That morning he'd heard on the radio that three goats had gone missing while crossing a bridge after Pittsburgh's Semiannual Sheepherder & Goat Jubilee. Carl reasoned a goat could get lost in a city it wasn't familiar with. But while crossing a bridge and surrounded by professional shepherds? It was a scandal that would be talked about for years (in certain goat-enthusiast circles). It felt like another reason for Carl to worry about monsters. So worry he did, while he stared over the truck's counter.

The Chesterfields had called a family meeting and agreed to all pitch in and give Mr. Chesterfield's dream a try. They'd need to work together to handle the flurry of customers that would show up for the grand opening. The prep work was completed the day before. Everything was neatly arranged in the refrigerator, available to be served that evening. The potato salad had been mixed. The creamy gravy for the chicken-fried steak sat ready to be drizzled. The blue cheese dressing previously poured into little bowls was still in little bowls, waiting to be placed next to salads. The picnic tables looked average. The food would be average, too. Mr. Chesterfield was thrilled. It was all as he'd planned—well, everything except for the sign. Carl's father had decided to open on a Wednesday so they could have a couple of days to ease into the taxing demands the weekend crowd would bring.

Carl watched as the neon sign flickered off and on every few seconds, illuminating the grass and the Ohio River. "The flickering gives the place character," rationalized Mr. Chesterfield. Carl smiled and nodded. He knew the sign would be better used if the truck had been rewired, but he couldn't bring himself to tell his father. The bridge floodlit purple. Then not. Then purple again.

As Carl stood at the ready, his mind wandered. He wanted the truck to be an instant success. If it was, they could keep their house. His father could be noble. His parents could be happy. Plus, life is always easier when things go well.

Carl peeked at his dad standing a few inches to his left in the cramped kitchen. His muscular arms crossed over his chest and his head held high, taking in the picnic tables across the counter. Carl had never seen his father so serious—a man who was constantly picking him up for impromptu piggyback rides, blissfully burped the alphabet on command, never went to work without a yo-yo in his glove compartment, and appeared unable to chew gum without blowing bubbles. Then Carl realized it wasn't seriousness he was reading on his father's face. It was pride. His father had built something that was his own. Something new. Something that could bring people together. Something that made Carl smile. Carl held that smile for who knows how long as his eyes drifted between his father, the spotless truck, and the empty picnic tables.

Eventually, Carl's smile curved into a frown as a bad feeling settled in. At first Carl wasn't sure what had caused his mood to change. Then all of a sudden it hit him—they were an hour into their grand opening and not a single customer had come to the counter. Carl's father looked devastated. His pride faded. His arms slumped by his sides. Carl knew his dad wanted the truck to open with a bang. Unfortunately, it was more of a whir, buzz, click, repeat.

His mother reached up through the truck's window and took his father's hand. The possibility of losing their old town house began to feel real. They needed to make enough money to cover the monthly payments on their home, the food truck, and the land, or they would lose all three. It occurred to Carl that just having one customer show up would increase their turnout infinitely. Basic math dictated. At any moment there were thousands of hungry people in Pittsburgh—couldn't one of them stumble by their food truck? Even someone looking for a quick snack?

Carl hoped.

And prayed.

And waited.

And waited some more.

Then the most beautiful sound in the world: footsteps on grass, as up walked the girl with the backward baseball cap.

Only she wasn't wearing her cap. Rather a blue blouse and black pants. Her hair in a ponytail. Eyes trained on the ground. A fashionable mother by her side.

Buzz. Click. Whir. Repeat. The purple light caused confusion, then shrugs.

Carl nearly gasped when he saw her. What luck! Whether it was good or bad remained to be seen. He reached toward a stack of laminated menus and grabbed a pair. His father promptly pulled them from his fingers before high-stepping out of the truck and handing them to the girl's mother. Not knowing what to do next, Carl crouched behind the counter. He immediately regretted the decision but decided to stay the course.

"Right this way, ladies." Mr. Chesterfield proudly walked toward the truck's best picnic table (the one closest to the bridge's beautiful near-tower, of course).

"Hi, Carl," the girl called before turning from the truck.

Not wanting to be impolite, Carl raised a hand and waved over the counter. Buzz. Click. Whir.

As Mrs. Chesterfield greeted the customers with waters, Mr. Chesterfield slipped back to Carl, who decided it was once again safe to stand.

"Do you have any idea who that is?"

Carl was baffled. How did his father know the girl with the backward baseball cap? "Um" was all he could muster.

"That's Maddy Lee. She writes a food column in the lifestyle section of the paper," proclaimed Mr. Chesterfield. "If she writes about this place, everyone in town will be talking about us. What are the chances?"

Carl asked himself the same question.

Then Carl held his breath and hoped for the best.

CHAPTER FOUR

H er feet hurt. She couldn't find her dress shoes, and her mother never let her wear sneakers when they reviewed restaurants, so she was forced to wear her size-and-a-half-too-small ballet flats from the previous year.

To make matters worse, her mother insisted they walk that evening. Fortunately, they only lived a half dozen blocks from the bridge. It felt good to sit, even on the hard wooden bench of a picnic table.

"I think there's a solid chance that my feet get squeezed off by dessert."

"I think you should clean your room so you can find your good shoes," said her mother. "It's a mess."

"I keep everything in piles on my floor so I know where it is."

"Everything except for your shoes."

"I didn't say it was a perfect system," she said with a shrug as she perused the menu.

It had taken her a moment to place Carl. But in fairness,

seeing anyone she knew behind a food truck counter beneath a bridge on a school night would be unexpected. And the crushing sensation around her feet made it difficult to focus. It even took her a couple of minutes to notice the lack of smell coming from the truck's kitchen.

Smells were the first things she clocked when dining at a new place. Before décor or service, it was always smell. Whether sweet, sour, spicy, savory, doughy, meaty, fishy, delicious, or disappointing, smells often gave away the type of meal she was in for before she and her mother walked through a door. But there was almost no smell coming from the truck's kitchen. Like there wasn't much going on in there. She pulled a small notepad and pencil from her pocket and scribbled a few quick thoughts to remind herself for later. Across the table, she watched her mother do something similar in her own notebook.

On the waitress's recommendation, she and her mother ordered the truck's house salad, chicken-fried steak, and potato salad. The family resemblance among Carl and the waitress and the man behind the counter made her smile. She always liked when she could tell people were related just by looking at them.

After trying the salad, she wrote the word *bland* on her notepad.

Lazy and *lukewarm* were her words for the chicken-fried steak.

And *aggressively boring* was what she jotted for the potato salad, followed by *sand?*

She felt bad about being critical of Carl's family's food truck but had to be honest with herself, too.

Every so often she looked over her shoulder. Each time she did, she caught Carl's eyes darting from her to the beautiful old bridge. He was funny, she thought. She wondered if he knew she was underwhelmed by the food. She also wondered how all those scratches got on the underside of the bridge.

Overall, the meal was average and uneventful. Then the check arrived.

Dreading the walk home, she leaned down to tug at the heels of her shoes. Maybe if she pulled hard enough they could stretch a size bigger? But as she leaned forward to take her shoes' elastic to the limit, she felt something rumble in her stomach. Like a pitcher of water was being poured from one side of her tummy to the other. Then back. The last time she'd felt that sensation was when she rode the Diablo Slingshot at the county fair, and she would never forget how that night ended.

Her eyes went wide and her hand shot to her mouth, pressing it shut. She bolted from her bench to the nearest trash can. Her mother didn't move quickly enough. Maddy Lee's dinner erupted out of her mouth and over the food truck's best picnic table.

Then the purple neon light clicked off again.

Electricity can be a funny thing. Not necessarily "funny ha-ha." More "funny peculiar." And as the electrician had warned, the food truck wasn't wired that well.

In the Chesterfields's truck, the electricity flowed from point A to point Z, hitting all the letters in between. Whenever that neon sign clicked off—let's call the sign point S—the electricity stopped flowing forward and started back at point A. But it would return with a vengeance, rushing to make up for lost time not spent at point Z. Literally at the speed of light, so one wouldn't notice that power had stopped flowing to anything other than the sign.

When that incredible avenging force had gone through the Chesterfields's fridge (point F, of course), it blew the refrigerator's fuse. With the fuse blown, the fridge no longer held electricity. But electricity still flowed through the rest of the vehicle. Moving from E to G, without powering F. Which of course caused the food in the fridge to spoil the night before the opening, and before it was served to Maddy Lee and her daughter.

It certainly wasn't "funny *ha-ha*." Unless electricity had a dark sense of humor.

The next day, Maddy Lee wrote about the truck in her column. It wasn't good.

There were no customers on Thursday. On Friday the sign gave out altogether.

Back home, Mrs. Chesterfield cooked in an effort to cheer up her husband. When she had first moved to Pittsburgh from Ohio, a friend from her dental class showed her how to make the local cuisine. Things like sandwiches and salads stuffed with fries and topped with eggs, burnt-almond tortes, square-cut pizza smothered with cold toppings, and pierogis, an eastern European dumpling of sorts. That night she made them all.

Unfortunately, Mr. Chesterfield was un-cheer-up-able. For the first time in Carl's life, his father barely touched his dinner.

"I just wanted to create something that was mine again," sighed Mr. Chesterfield as he gazed at the mound of food on this plate. "Maybe I'm dreaming too big."

Carl had more trouble sleeping than ever that night. He was concerned about his father, and the girl, and worried about his family's home. Also, his parents were arguing loudly. He wrote a little to try to get some of his heavier thoughts out, but he still felt anxious. So he went to his window and counted the thirty-three bridges. They stood firm, which made him feel a little better. But not enough to stop worrying about everything else on his mind.

Mrs. Chesterfield knocked on his door and poked her head in. "Saw your light on. Sorry we were so loud."

Carl gave her a weak smile.

"Don't worry, kiddo. It'll all work out."

He nodded. Got back into bed. But his worries and uncertainties didn't go away.

"But how?" he asked.

"Wonderful things can happen in this world, Carl. You can't give up hope." Mrs. Chesterfield shut off the light. "Wonderful things."

CHAPTER FIVE

Maddy Lee hadn't majored in journalism to write op-ed columns and reviews. She'd planned to be an investigative journalist. Sure, she'd rather seek out local corruption, or report on the dark unknowns of the city, but being an investigative journalist was how she viewed her work reviewing Pittsburgh's newest food establishments. She knew she was lying to herself, but to be fair, her investigative background was how she was able to find Chesterfields's hidden away beneath a bridge. Maddy treasured her work, her daughter, and her readers.

Maddy Lee's readers cherished her insight. She was blunt and honest. And her taste was impeccable. If Maddy Lee said something was great, then it was great. If she said it was awful, it was awful. There was never any gray with Maddy. Everything was either day or night, good or bad, hot or cold. To the people of Pittsburgh, her opinion was as good as fact. So, after Maddy wrote that Chesterfields's "reeked of uninspired blandness that was only remotely interesting when coming back up," that was what her readers thought, too.

And unfortunately for the Chesterfields, everyone in Pittsburgh read Maddy Lee.

By Saturday it was clear that Mr. Chesterfield knew he needed to do something drastic. Things would have to be shaken up if the family was going to keep their old town house.

Mrs. Chesterfield agreed. "Why don't you sell the truck?"

Carl watched his father hopefully as the man pondered.

"You're right," Mr. Chesterfield announced.

"I am?" Mrs. Chesterfield wondered aloud as Mr. Chesterfield grabbed Carl's hand and charged out of the town house to make the long walk to their quarter acre of land under a bridge.

"We're going to sell the truck," Mr. Chesterfield proclaimed.

"Uh, great," said Carl, surprised how easily his father had come to his senses.

"Really get the word out. Go door-to-door and explain why people should be eating at our new and improved food truck."

The boy's face fell. "Oh. That kind of selling."

"Don't worry, Carl. I have a plan. A secret one."

It didn't sound like the best idea, but Carl forced himself to smile and nod as his father continued.

"I hatched it reading Maddy Lee's review for the seventeenth time. I mean, I didn't need an article to tell me something wasn't right. Obviously, *I* couldn't be to blame for anything that went wrong. But then, who? Suddenly it hit me: It's the food. Not just that it was spoiled. It was too fancy! And who needs table service at a food truck? People should order at the counter. We need things that speak to the *average* person."

Carl sighed. It didn't seem worthwhile to remind his father that he'd set the menu and established the service and ordering protocols himself. But he did like the idea of thinking of chicken-fried steak as fancy.

"So, we're revamping and relaunching," said Mr. Chesterfield. "Just a simple menu. Well-done hamburgers. Egg salad sandwiches. Fries. Average food for average folks."

"Um, super."

"Isn't it?" said Mr. Chesterfield with a smile.

Before long, Carl and his father made it to the bridge and split up to get the word out about the reopening. Carl took a deep breath before knocking on the door of a neighboring linen factory.

"Need help with something?" asked the hairnetted woman who poked her head out.

But Carl just stood there. Because he didn't know.

On Sunday, aside from the neon sign being removed, the truck looked the same.

"I assumed you'd go back to work," fretted Mrs. Chesterfield as she packed the leftover ingredients from the original menu into her car.

"I am back to work," said Mr. Chesterfield, happily wiping the food truck with a sponge.

Carl offered to help with the food prep. When he wasn't worrying about monsters, he was thinking more and more about food. He appreciated that it could make people happy and healthy. He'd also come to appreciate the benefits of proper refrigeration. He suggested toasting the bread for the sandwiches, but his father thought toasted bread with egg salad was a little adventurous for the average customer. Carl hard-boiled a few dozen eggs instead.

They would reopen for lunch the following day. Things were back on track(ish) for the Chesterfields as they went off to bed. Everything exactly where Carl's father wanted.

Until somehow, during the night, the food truck with the busted engine and blown tires moved twenty feet.

CHAPTER SIX

I t must be neighborhood kids," surmised Mr. Chesterfield as they drove by the repositioned food truck the next morning. "Always moving food trucks in the middle of the night for fun. It's too close to the picnic tables now. Kind of makes the quarter of an acre feel like a tenth of an acre. I'll call a tow truck to move it back."

Carl wasn't sure his dad knew what neighborhood kids did for fun. But in all fairness, he wasn't sure either. Being in no position to question his father, he wished him luck on the truck's relaunch and walked into the timeworn brick schoolhouse.

Carl also wasn't sure if anyone at school had realized he had been gone for two weeks. It was like his invisibility had returned. No one sat next to him in class. No one even snickered at his hair in the hall. At first Carl was too busy worrying about the girl with the backward baseball cap to notice. He desperately wanted to apologize and make sure she was okay, but unfortunately, she was nowhere to be found.

By third period, Carl had crawled out of his head and was

observing others again. Arguably, things weren't much different than before his suspension. But for some reason, he now felt lonelier than ever. He wanted to be noticed, or at least acknowledged. Sadly, the only way to change things would be for Carl to reach out. But what if the other kids laughed? What if they didn't care what he had to say?

Carl tried to catch the gaze of anyone he saw during lunch. But anyone he locked eyes with would quickly look away. Everyone except for Principal Wilkinson—Principal Wilkinson gave him the evil eye. A generous helping of it.

Carl's anxiety built. His breathing sped up. He swore he could feel the blood flowing through his veins. As it started to feel too much for him, he saw Teddy, the skinny, freckled kid with the windbreaker, watching him across the cafeteria. He gave a

friendly wave, but the kid just kept staring. So Carl did his best to ignore him and eat. He was moderately successful.

Carl was emotionally drained when the last school bell rang. He slowly gathered his things and headed for the door. At the end of the hall he saw the girl with the backward baseball cap in front of the bulletin board. Then she made for the exit.

He hurried down the crowded hallway after her, but by the time he stepped from the building she was nowhere in sight. He sighed, then became curious. Walked back to the bulletin board. Among many thumbtacked announcements was a taped flyer on turquoise paper:

THE MIDNIGHT BRIGADE

FIRST MEETING TONIGHT AT 11:15.

MEET AT THE STREET CORNER UNDER THE RED AWNING.

YES, THIS FLYER IS SPECIFICALLY DIRECTED AT <u>YOU</u>.

("YOU" MEANING "CARL")

After dinner that night, Carl headed to the food truck to help his father clean. He held the flyer with two hands, reading it again and again on the way.

She had reached out to him, he thought with a smile. She had recovered from the food poisoning. She remembered the awning where they had their first proper chat. And The MB *had* to be the Midnight Brigade.

Then new questions emerged: How did she know he would see the flyer? Did she know he was looking for her? Did she expect him to fight monsters with her? Did this mean she had been thinking of him, too? Ah, the mysteries of the universe.

Mr. Chesterfield served his final well-done hamburger an hour before Carl arrived at the truck. Customers had come that day. Just not many (though no one projectile-vomited, which was progress). They were average folks, and they had average meals. Mr. Chesterfield felt noble, but he knew he'd have to do better to keep the old town house. Business would need to improve, he explained to his son. They needed to target more customers, like those ads in the paper had targeted him. But advertising in the paper was too expensive. He was convinced there must be another way to notify potential customers about their food truck.

"We could put up flyers," offered Carl.

Mr. Chesterfield shook his head and smiled at his son. "Flyers. The classified ads of the average man."

The idea was perfect. It was inspired (by the girl with the backward cap, specifically). Carl was proud to contribute. Proud that his father liked it. As Mr. Chesterfield began cleaning, Carl thought that maybe things would be all right. But worry soon overtook Carl once more as a realization settled in: he would need to sneak out of his house at eleven o'clock that night. How on earth would he manage that?

CHAPTER SEVEN

Teddy had been covered in freckles as long as he could remember. Usually, they didn't bother him. He often saw them as a helpful identifying characteristic, since so many people referred to him as "the kid with all the freckles."

When Teddy was in third grade, some older boys convinced him that if he played connect-the-dots with his freckles a hidden image would appear. Unfortunately, he just ended up with a face covered in blue ink and a profound regret that he'd used a permanent marker. It took a week of daily scrubbing before Teddy stopped looking like a blueberry.

Teddy's father wasn't upset with him for coloring his face. But he was furious with the other boys for taking advantage of his naive son. His father never blamed him for anything. The boy could do no wrong in his eyes, which was one of the reasons the two of them had such a great relationship. Historically, Teddy's strongest relationships were with people who had at least a decade on him in age. Usually much more.

Mrs. Bigelsen, for instance, had been one of his closest confidants for years. Sure, she was his father's secretary and had grandchildren in high school, but her grandkids didn't appreciate knitting as much as she and Teddy did.

And there was Marvin, the shoeshine guy down the block from Teddy's building. Teddy and Marvin had been chewing each other's ears off since before Teddy knew how to tie his laces.

And who could forget Ms. Sanchez, across the hall from their apartment? Their friendship started after she hired him to pick up her newspaper when she was out of town, though it blossomed after they began reading that paper together on Sunday mornings while drinking herbal tea.

But Teddy's best friend was his sister, Veronica. Their father was older than most parents when Teddy came into the world, and their parents divorced shortly after. Growing up, Teddy idolized his dad, but his sister was the one who took him to the park, and to swim practice, and listened to his jokes, and heard his concerns, and generally taught him how to function as a young Pittsburgher. She was patient and kind and smart and funny. Teddy's older sister was his favorite person on the planet—and now she was miles away at college.

It was Veronica who told her baby brother during one of their weekly phone calls (always a bright spot of Teddy's week) that he should try to develop friendships with kids his own age. The process was slow and riddled with misguided attempts.

There was the Leprechaun Appreciation Club. Teddy was the only member but quit after he lost the election to be the organization's vice president. For nearly a year, Teddy tried to launch the Society for Friendship Between Children and Ghosts. But he eventually gave up because no one else ever came to the meetings (at least he was pretty sure no one ever came).

He'd probably throw in the towel on his latest endeavor, too, if no one joined soon, but it would take dumb luck, a wild misunderstanding, or some kind of miracle for that to happen.

Teddy zipped up his windbreaker and hoped for dumb luck.

————◆————

Carl counted the thirty-three bridges thirty-three times that evening. He could draw the view outside his window from memory if he needed to. He was sure of it. He wasn't sure how or why that would ever be necessary, but he was sure just the same.

Carl was nervous. Concerned that he'd get caught. Uneasy that he could get hurt. Worried that she might not show.

His plan was simple—he'd seen it in countless movies. He would tie his bedsheets together and climb out his second-story window. No more than thirteen or so feet down, he figured.

But what if he slipped? He'd surely twist an ankle.

What if the sheets came loose? He'd likely break his legs.

And what if someone spotted the bedsheet rope out his window while he was gone? He'd undoubtedly be grounded (though that probably wouldn't change his life in any noticeable way).

He spent nearly an hour tying his sheets together. Pulling them as tight as he could. Making certain the knots would hold. And then he spent another half hour perfecting the knot that attached the end of the sheets to the radiator.

By 10:59 he was certain the sheets were tied as strongly as could be. But that didn't make him any less nervous. Looking out his window to the pavement below didn't help. He'd simply have to go for it. If he waited much longer he'd be late. Maybe a quick trip to the bathroom first? He didn't have to go, but he had a minute or so. Might as well try.

As Carl tiptoed from his room, he saw that the lights were out in the rest of the house. Then it occurred to him that he hadn't heard his parents arguing for a couple of hours—they were asleep, like they tended to be every night around this time.

Carl took a deep breath, snuck downstairs, and walked out the front door.

It was a flawless escape.

———◆———

Teddy pulled the windbreaker's orange hood over his floppy red curls. It was colder than he'd expected, but he had promised himself he'd give it one last try.

So he shivered.

And waited.

Hopefully.

Then less hopefully.

Then hopefully again.

And then, right on time, he saw a figure about his size turn the corner at the end of the block. Teddy bit his tongue to stop smiling. He was ecstatic, but this was serious business. He watched as the figure's arms hugged its body. He should have worn a sweatshirt, Teddy thought.

———————◆———————

"I should've worn a sweatshirt," Carl mumbled to himself.

Then he looked up and saw Teddy, the odd kid from school, standing under the red awning. Carl's shoulders slumped. When he'd run through all the things that could go wrong that evening, he'd overlooked the possibility that the flyers weren't from the girl with the backward baseball cap at all. He cupped his hands over his mouth and blew into them like he'd seen cold people do on street corners. It didn't make him any warmer.

"I was hoping you'd come," said Teddy.

It was then that Carl realized that he had never spoken to Teddy. No time like the present.

"What's the, uh, Midnight Brigade?"

"Well, so far it's only me. But I was thinking you could join? Then there would be two of us. Closer to a proper brigade, right?"

"Oh. But what is it exactly?"

"An investigative collective sworn to protect several hundred of Pittsburgh's grandest treasures."

Carl scratched his head, then hugged his chest again to warm up.

"I'm, um, still not sure I'm following you."

"Sorry. Thought you might've been able to put it together from my first flyer." Teddy took a deep breath. Then he became very, very serious. "I think monsters are eating our bridges, Carl."

Carl's face dropped. There it was—his deep fear verbalized. So Carl asked the only thing a boy in his position could ask:

"Are you sure?"

"That seems to be the most likely reason for the damage that's been done to structures that would typically be considered architecturally indestructible. Chunks of steel are being torn from our bridges. I mean, if it's not monsters, your guess is as good as mine."

Carl didn't have a better guess.

"It's just…" Carl trailed off. Hearing it out loud made him feel ridiculous for worrying about monsters in the first place. After all, he'd practically been sleep-deprived when he thought he saw that bridge move. How to phrase this delicately? "It's just…" he continued. "Just, um, that no one has seen any monsters."

"That's why the Midnight Brigade needs you, Carl. I've watched you. You're like me. You're an observer. You see things other people don't. If anyone is gonna see a monster it'll be us."

Carl wasn't so sure. "Right… Thank you?"

"You're welcome."

Carl tapped his chin with his index finger. "Why doesn't the, um, Midnight Brigade meet at midnight?"

"Don't you think that'd be a little expected? We're a secret society. We need to be unpredictable."

"Got it."

"You're skeptical, I know. It's okay. I get and appreciate that. Skepticism is important. That's why I'm not running around screaming 'Monsters are eating our bridges!' Sure, I maybe implied that between the lines on a flyer. But that was just to get your attention, and I can't imagine anyone else would've made the leap that 'something is ravaging' meant 'monsters are eating.' We need to be smart about this. We need to see a monster with our own eyes, and *then* we can go running around screaming. It's the civil thing to do."

"Uh-huh."

"I'm losing you, aren't I?"

"Uh. No."

"It's okay. Baby steps. Look, I think this is a cause that you're gonna get behind. Just do me one favor? Go to your favorite bridge tonight and give it some good, hard, thoughtful observation. Think about how devastated you'd be if something happened to it. Then think about how much force it would take to rip a chunk out of that bridge. Monsters are the only logical explanation. Our bridges are counting on us. Don't let your bridge down, Carl."

———◆———

The more Carl thought about it as he headed home alone, the sillier he felt. It was delusional to believe monsters existed in Pittsburgh. And Teddy seemed a little nuts. But if he had the same theories as Teddy, wouldn't that make him nuts, too? That said, he didn't want to hurt Teddy's feelings or disappoint him. People rarely asked anything of Carl, and in the grand scheme of things, this wasn't a "big ask." He'd spend some time looking at his favorite bridge and then go home. Easy as that.

But which bridge was his favorite? Carl loved bridges. He'd never had to pick a favorite before. Pittsburgh had so many amazing options. The Roberto Clemente Bridge. The Hot Metal Bridge. Fort Pitt Bridge. Panther Hollow Bridge. It would be like asking a parent to pick their favorite child. That wasn't that hard for the Chesterfields (Carl being an only child and all), but parents with two or more kids? Impossible. There were over four hundred bridges to choose from and they were all the best in their own way.

Carl moseyed toward the family's old town house as he wrestled with the complexities of the most difficult decision any Pittsburgher ever had to make. Before he knew it, he was passing the bridge next to his father's food truck. Instantly, he knew it was his favorite. Not only was it a gorgeous suspension bridge built by his great-grandfather, but his family now owned a quarter acre of land below it. He would stare at the bridge and then go home. It would be a job well done for Teddy, and then he could forget about the whole thing.

The boy wandered under the bridge. Passed that big pile of rocks and his father's food truck. Took a seat on a patch of grass. He'd gotten used to the temperature and could appreciate the crisp night air as he marveled at the steel construction. All the shops in the area had been closed for hours, so there wasn't a soul in sight. It was a little piece of heaven in Pittsburgh on a full-moon night. And as far as Carl could tell, it was absolutely monster-free.

But how long would he have to wait until he could honestly

tell Teddy he'd given it a real shot? Five minutes? Eleven? Carl had school in the morning, and if he got home soon he could still get close to seven hours of sleep. He'd gotten by on less before, but why push it? Surely spending nine minutes looking for monsters on a bridge was a solid effort from a sane observer. Carl frowned at his watch. Yes, he'd give it three more minutes before heading home.

And as long as he was here, he figured he might as well get comfortable. So he'd laid on the grass, hands behind his head. It was quiet, with only the gentle musings of the Ohio River. Soothing. Carl's eyes fluttered, then shut.

Sometime later he jolted awake.

Fifteen minutes? Three hours? There was no telling how long he'd been out.

It was still dark. It took Carl a few moments to get his bearings, to figure out why he wasn't in his second-story bedroom. Right, the bridge! It looked just as he'd left it.

Carl stumbled to his feet. Time to go home. But something was off. The food truck had moved six or seven yards closer to the picnic tables. And the pile of rocks that had been two school buses high was now scattered across the ground.

Then the night got darker, like someone had shut off the moon.

Carl looked up, and for a split second his heart stopped.

Gazing down at him was a giant.

The boy screamed, but no sound came out.

CHAPTER EIGHT

T he giant wasn't traditionally handsome. Traditionally unat-
tractive, sure, but not handsome. He stood twenty-five
feet tall. Had massive biceps and a potbelly that made his
torso pear-shaped. His legs were short and stubby, his nose and
ears exaggerated and crusty. His shoes and tunic were made of
leather. And his teeth were yellow and covered in plaque. This
was someone who absolutely did not floss twice a day (or probably ever).

Carl's mouth had never been more open.

And the giant had never been more confused.

"This is embarrassing," said the giant. "I didn't notice you
there. People aren't really supposed to see me." His voice was
gruff, but quieter than one would expect.

"You're not gonna eat the bridge, are you?"

"Wh-why would I—" The giant threw his hands in the air.
"Why would I eat the bridge?"

Carl shuffled his feet. The whole idea felt sillier than ever now, even with the creature standing over him. "I, um, heard monsters were eating our bridges."

"Monsters? You think I'm a monster? Do you have any idea how offensive that is? Think I'm going to eat the bridge... Unbelievable."

"So, you're, uh, not a monster?"

The giant shook his head. Took a deep breath. Collected himself.

"I'm a troll, kid."

Carl nodded. Did his best to accept the answer. "Oh. Sure."

"Haven't you ever seen a troll before?"

"Sounds like I'm not supposed to."

"Fair. Yeah, I do try to stay hidden. But people talk about me, right? I mean, arguably a troll wouldn't be great for tourism, but I like to think that me living here is a big part of what makes Pittsburgh, Pittsburgh."

"Sorry."

"Not your fault," he sighed. "I'm Frank."

"Frank? Frank the troll?"

"Just Frank."

"Seems like a funny name for a troll."

Frank's head snapped back. Stung by the slight.

"And what do you think a good name for a troll would be?"

Carl gave it some thought. "Frank's good enough, I guess."

"Good enough... Thanks, kid. Big of you."

"I'm Carl."

Frank sighed. Stuck out a gigantic hand. "Nice to meet you."

Carl examined the hand, then wrapped his own around one of Frank's fingers and shook.

"So, you're, uh, not here to destroy the bridge?"

Frank pressed his lips together.

"Listen. I don't do it anymore, but I spent my entire career *protecting* bridges."

"From what?"

"Invading hordes. Mythological beasts. General decay."

Carl nodded. It seemed like the right kind of job for a troll to have.

"I think, um, something has been taking bites out of our bridges."

Frank took a step back, then kicked the ground with his foot. "Well, I'm sure that's over with," he mumbled. "But like I said, I don't protect bridges anymore."

"So, do you, like, eat people who cross the bridge?"

"Are you trying to hurt my feelings? One troll eats one guy on a bridge and we never hear the end of it. And I knew that guy. Not a nice dude. He didn't even taste good."

"Wait. How do you know what he tasted like?"

Frank threw his arms in the air again. "Okay! I ate one guy.

But he was a total jerk and it was a lapse in judgment. I didn't enjoy it and it won't happen again."

Carl nodded. He wasn't sure why, but he believed the troll.

"Did you, uh, eat those missing goats?"

"I'm a troll! Cut me some slack."

"Right. So, you're gonna be here for a while?"

The troll shrugged. "Maybe. Hard to tell."

"Can I, um, ask a favor?"

The troll's head snapped back again. "Favor? Yeah, I guess you can ask..."

"Could you, uh, maybe stop moving my dad's food truck?"

"Food truck? Oh, that thing?" The troll pointed to the truck. "I stub my toe on that every time I wake up from my rock pile."

"You sleep under rocks?"

"Yeah, why? You think I'm just gonna sleep under the bridge? I'm not an animal. Besides, people would see me."

"Oh. Right. Well, uh, do you think maybe you could put the truck back where it was and be a little more careful when you wake up from now on?"

The troll snorted. Nodded. "Sure. Whatever. Nothing would make me happier. 'Be more careful'! It's *my* toe...I'm fine, by the way."

"Oh. Okay. Thanks."

"I'm gonna need a favor from you, too."

"Really?"

"Yeah. Kind of an important one." The troll looked around, then leaned in conspiratorially. "Do you think you could keep me secret?"

The boy smiled. He knew he could. It was in his blood.

CHAPTER NINE

Sneaking into the town house was as easy as sneaking out. Staying awake the next day was another matter.

Carl had gotten home much later than he'd anticipated. Worse, he had trouble falling asleep when he got to his bed. Thoughts of Frank kept him up (as world-altering discoveries tend to do). Even remaining conscious at breakfast was tough. Luckily his parents hardly noticed. Mrs. Chesterfield was buried in the family's finances, wrapping her head around bank and mortgage statements, becoming more stressed the more she read. And Mr. Chesterfield proudly boasted (to anyone who might be listening) about what an unbelievable day it would be to sell hamburgers and egg salad sandwiches. He had plastered the neighborhood with flyers and would have new customers by the busload.

Carl dozed in class for most of Tuesday morning. But his being small and unpopular allowed his slumber to go unnoticed. Around noon, the lunch bell jerked him awake. Though hazy at the edges, his memories from the previous night were fairly firm in his mind (details of dreams tended to be fluid). He could still vividly picture Frank's oversized crusty nose and leather ensemble, and hear his voice when he'd asked to keep him a secret.

As Carl stepped into the hallway, he was greeted with a *pssst*. He turned to find an eager Teddy. Carl hadn't given much thought to what he'd say to him.

"Well?" asked the boy in the orange windbreaker, doing his best to keep his excitement down. "How was your bridge? Did you see anything?"

Carl decided to choose his words carefully.

"The, um, bridge was fine."

It wasn't a lie—the bridge itself was fine. Perhaps it was a lie of omission. And on the morality scale, that seemed to be a step closer to good than bad.

Teddy nodded. "Yeah. Mine too. Not a single monster. That's three hundred and seventeen nights in a row. Every night I've checked has been one hundred percent monster-free."

Carl cringed. Began to feel guilty. But then he remembered trolls and monsters aren't the same thing. Sure, it was a technicality, but a technicality is a technicality.

Teddy sighed. "So, does this mean you're not going to join the Midnight Brigade? I totally understand if you want to back out. I mean, I guess you were never really all the way in, so you can't really back out, but you get what I'm saying."

"Maybe I could, uh, be a secret member?"

Teddy's face lit up. "Yeah? Excellent! And totally in line with the spirit of the organization!" The skinny boy stared off at nothing in particular. He seemed pleased with himself. Delighted by the growth of his secret society. Thrilled with the possibilities to come.

"Um. Okay," said Carl.

"Yeah, well, see you around! I'll be here when you need me. You know, to exchange notes. Provide insight. Whatever you need. Consider me at your disposal."

Carl gave him a hearty nod and made his way to lunch.

He would eat alone.

———◆———

After school Carl wanted to crawl into bed, but before he'd left the house that morning he had sleepily promised his father he'd swing by the food truck. So he semireluctantly made his way toward his favorite bridge. He wanted to be a good son, and, selfishly, he wanted to get a closer look at that rock pile in the daylight. He wondered if he could see the troll buried under it. The pile was massive, but so was Frank. And once Carl started thinking about Frank, he couldn't stop. Why had the troll retired from protecting bridges? Was Pittsburgh in danger? Was his father's food truck going to be okay?

His head elsewhere, he nearly tripped over a leg sticking out into the sidewalk. It belonged to the girl with the backward baseball cap. She leaned against the steps of a magnificent brownstone.

"Sorry. Didn't see you there."

Carl regained his composure. "No, uh, problem." His lips curled into a smile as he noticed the doodles decorating her once-white sneakers. Her left shoe had dozens of pirates swordfighting what appeared to be the British Navy. And on the right shoe, the sun setting over Pittsburgh.

She smirked. He needed to say something else. He realized he still owed her an apology.

"I'm sorry we made you sick."

"Don't be. That's the most excitement my mom and I have had all year."

"Oh. Well, you're welcome?"

Her smile grew. "We can call it even."

Carl looked puzzled.

"For the suspension?"

"Oh."

"I'm Bertha. But everyone calls me Bee."

"Uh, Carl."

"We've established that, Carl."

"Right." Carl gently tapped his toes on the pavement. "Wait. You're *Bee Lee*?" he said, liking the sound of her name.

"Why?"

"No reason. It's just, uh, great," he stammered. And he meant it. Because it was.

"Agreed." She smiled. "So, how's chef life? Have you gotten dangerous and tried toasting pumpernickel or sourdough?"

"I've, um, taken a step back from toast. Focusing on hard-boiled eggs now. Just add eggs to boiling water. Then, uh, remove, peel, and eat. Fewer steps."

"You're at least using salt and pepper, right?"

Carl drew a blank.

"For seasoning?"

Carl's cheeks turned red.

"Flavor, Carl. Flavor."

"Oh. Um. I'll have to try that."

Bee shook her head. "You have so much to learn."

"You know a lot about food, don't you?"

"My mom's taken me to almost every restaurant in town. A girl picks things up."

Carl nodded, then yawned.

"Sorry to bore you," she said with a smile.

"Oh! Uh, no! It's just that I was out until three last night . . ."

"Secret mission?"

"Well, kinda." Carl scratched the back of his head. "Maybe I could show you?"

Bee's right eyebrow went up.

CHAPTER TEN

B ee was the youngest person in the city to travel across all of Pittsburgh's bridges. It wasn't a goal she had set out to achieve, or even an accomplishment she was aware of. Just something that came naturally from her mother driving her all over town on the back of her moped to review restaurants, food trucks, carts, and stands.

Indian, Polish, Japanese, Cambodian, Italian, Ethiopian, Chinese, Peruvian, Hungarian? Name a cuisine and Bee could tell you her three favorite places to eat within a twenty-minute ride. And by taking those rides with her mother, Bee fell in love with the bridges that got them where they were going.

In addition to her mother's silky black hair and love of food, Bee Lee had inherited Maddy's passion for investigation. Bee talked to everyone. Especially servers, chefs, hosts, valets, dishwashers, and bartenders who hung out in front of the restaurants in the dicier parts of town. The dishwashers had the best gossip. The stories that the tabloids weren't even digging into. Like the colossal creature that was spotted under a bridge on

Grandview Avenue. Newspapers wouldn't touch that stuff. But Bee had it on good authority that while they were on break, two dishwashers and a bartender saw that entire bridge shake when the creature brushed its shoulder against it. People in the service industry always knew what was really going on in Pittsburgh. And Bee did, too, because she listened to them. So when Carl said he wanted to show her something under a bridge, he had her attention.

In the afternoon sun, the rock pile near Carl's food truck looked like a rock pile. The beanbag-sized stones were stacked at least three layers deep. Bee wasn't immediately impressed. And she wasn't sure why Carl had brought her here. But she was surer than ever that Carl had one of the worst haircuts she had ever seen.

She watched him staring intently into the rocks beside her, his mouth moving slightly. Bee figured he did this when he was deciding what to say. She wished he'd say *something*. Give some sort of clue as to what they were doing here. What was she doing with Carl anyway? It had been a fluke that she slid into that empty seat next to him in the cafeteria. But perhaps not a total fluke. There had only been two empty seats in the entire cafeteria, and they were both next to Carl.

Why was he so quiet? Was he waiting on her to talk? Was he

mad at her? Disappointed? Was he expecting her to notice something absolutely incredible and right in front of her face?

What was she missing?

She looked harder into the rocks. Squinted a little. Then opened her eyes as wide as they would go. What was she supposed to be seeing?

Just rocks, as far as she could tell.

And a boy with an unfortunate haircut who wasn't talking.

Bee began to think she should manage her time better.

So after a while she left with a shrug and an "I've got homework."

The troll had done a fine job of covering himself. So fine that Carl wondered if he was even under there. He wasn't sure what he'd intended to show Bee, but he was certain she'd seen less than she expected.

Carl felt bad about breaking Frank's trust by bringing Bee. Worse, he felt ashamed for bringing Bee but not Teddy. Clearly his parents were better at managing secrets than he was. And worst of all, he felt bad about awkwardly staring at a pile of rocks with the girl he liked and not saying a word. Perhaps he should have explained more before they began staring at the rock pile together. Her frown suggested she didn't buy his trust-me-this-will-be-incredible-and-so-worth-your-time-you-just-need-to-see-these-rocks-with-me story. That or Carl needed to start wearing deodorant.

Either way, he was crushed when she left.

But what could he have done differently?

He wanted to tell her how wonderful his memories of Frank were from the night before. How Frank had coarse hair growing from his ears and a vague scent of blue cheese. How when Frank's belly growled the ground rumbled. How Frank had spent his life valiantly defending bridges before retiring to Pittsburgh. How Frank had asked him not to tell anyone about him, but how he trusted Bee and suspected Frank would, too.

He wanted to tell her about his parents and what life was like growing up in the old town house. And that he loved seeing his father happy. That he worried his father's pursuit of happiness might cause them to lose their home. And that he often saw things differently than his dad did but didn't want to hurt his feelings. That he wondered if keeping his opinions to himself made him feel more alone.

He wanted to tell her about planning to leaf through some cookbooks. About wanting to know more for his father and himself. About paying more attention to food because of her. About all the time he'd spent thinking about her and how that made him smile.

Instead he said nothing and regretted it.

Carl sighed, then stepped away to visit his dad.

Mr. Chesterfield believed the day had gone adequately. "Normally having an adequate day is perfectly fine, but when you start your day thinking it'll be unbelievable, only having an adequate day is a disaster. Setting reasonable expectations is important," he explained.

It was hard for Carl to disagree.

The flyers had brought in a dozen or so new customers. Young and old. Fat and skinny. Long- and short-haired. Raúl from the shoe shop. Tina from the bakery. Arman from the grocery store. Mr. Chesterfield appreciated meeting new folks. He was reaching all kinds of people in the neighborhood. But then he made a troubling observation: he didn't recognize a single face from the previous day. When you have a limited number of customers, you remember all their faces. He was aware that most people don't eat at the same place two days in a row. But if no one was coming back, maybe it was cause for concern. Sometimes the biggest problem with a problem is knowing whether you have a problem at all.

"We're gonna need to have repeat business," Mr. Chesterfield told his son.

Carl looked around the food truck at the cartons and cartons of uncooked eggs and unopened bags of buns.

"Do you think the prices are too high?" asked Carl.

Mr. Chesterfield examined his menu. Everything seemed reasonable. More importantly, "We're not even making a profit off the prices we have now. I was thinking we'd establish a customer base and then slowly raise prices over time. Get 'em hooked before we start charging what we deserve."

Carl nodded. It sounded wise. Potentially.

"Maybe we, um, put up more flyers?" offered Carl.

"Can't hurt. But I'm not sure it'll address the problem. If there is one."

"Oh." Carl thought harder until an idea struck him. "Maybe we could, um, write a letter to see if the City Celebration parade could, uh, include the neighborhood on its route? It's less than four weeks away. It could, uh, jump-start business?"

Mr. Chesterfield shook his head. "We're too far on the outskirts of downtown. There's no way they'd ever have the parade come by here. Don't waste your time." He sighed. "What would make you eat at the same place two days in a row?"

"I eat in the cafeteria at school every day."

"Good. But probably not an apples-to-apples comparison."

Carl nodded. Glanced at the giant pile of rocks. What would people think if they knew there was a troll living under this bridge? Maybe that would encourage folks to come take a look—mobs of them. And people get hungry. The only place to eat under the bridge was the food truck. But on the other hand, Frank might scare off the few customers Carl's father had.

"There has to be something we can do to get customers to come back," said Mr. Chesterfield as he folded a flyer into a paper airplane and flung it across the kitchen.

Carl looked at a well-done hamburger and a basket of cold French fries.

"Maybe if our food was really, really good?"

"If only it were that simple."

That evening Carl wrote to the organizers of City Celebration anyway. He told them how much he loved Pittsburgh, how special his bridge was, and how much heart and pride his dad poured into his food truck and his neighborhood. He dropped the letter in the mail before eating dinner with his mother.

When Carl was little, most evenings and afternoons after his mom got off work it was just the two of them. As he grew, they spent less and less time together. Things like school, television programs, and homework got in the way. Which made them sad, but neither of them said anything (as family members often do not).

Now that his father was dealing with the truck at dinnertime and no longer needed help with table service, perhaps Mrs. Chesterfield would get to spend more alone time with her son.

Mrs. Chesterfield was a decent cook. And the kitchen in the old town house was one of Carl's favorite rooms in their home. It was cozy. And he thought it had a nice smell. Not the smell of lingering food, the way some kitchens smell like fish or steak from the previous night. But of oak (which the kitchen's island was made of) and lemon (which was used to clean the oak).

His mother made her pierogis. A staple of the Pittsburgh culinary world and a wonderful comfort food. There's nothing better than having comfort food in a cozy kitchen. And while most of Mrs. Chesterfield's food was pretty good, the pierogis were the exception. They were spectacular.

Pierogis are prepared by creating thin, two-inch slices of dough, which are laid on top of each other and meshed into little pockets filled with mashed potatoes, ground meat, or cheese (Mrs. Chesterfield liked to use a little of all three). Then they're pressed shut and boiled in hot water (like raviolis). After they're boiled, they're typically topped with some combination of butter, sauerkraut, and sour cream. Carl liked to use butter (and lots of it). But Mrs. Chesterfield had a secret step just before. After the pierogis finished boiling, she'd fry them on the stove for a minute, which gave them a little extra char and texture. When Carl was younger, she used to tell him that this step was called "adding the love."

As Carl ate, he thought about how much he loved his mother. As Mrs. Chesterfield watched him eat, she thought about how much she loved her son. Not a word was spoken until Carl said, "Good night."

———◆———

By 1:17 a.m. it was clear that Carl couldn't sleep. Being tired all day and then not being able to fall asleep afterward was one of his least-favorite things. It had been happening often, and when it did, time moved at a snail's pace. There was usually something to blame for it, a cause that Carl could point his finger to. Worry about a test. Excitement for a holiday. Concern for his parents. Or in this case, rampant thoughts about a troll living under a bridge.

With sleep nowhere in sight, Carl kicked off his covers, threw on a hoodie, and walked to his father's food truck. He strolled under the bridge to find the rock pile still standing two school buses tall. The boy approached the pile, leaned in, and whispered:

"Uh, Frank?"

Nothing. Just rocks being rocks.

"Are you in there?"

If he was, the rocks wouldn't say.

"I'm just gonna, uh, wait a minute or so for you to come out. It's Carl, by the way."

Carl watched and waited. He tried poking a couple of rocks, but it didn't seem to make a difference. Maybe he had dreamt the whole thing. The more he thought about it, the more he decided that was the most likely explanation. A dream made so much more sense than a troll living alongside the Ohio River. Perhaps it *was* neighborhood kids who moved his father's truck and damaged those other bridges? Shenanigans and what have you.

The thought brought Carl peace. And with the rock pile not going anywhere, he went home and snuck into bed.

Carl slept well.

So well that he overslept.

CHAPTER ELEVEN

The next morning, Mr. Chesterfield was up and out the door with his weed whacker before Carl typically woke up. He planned to tidy up the patches of grass around the picnic tables before customers arrived. Because if there's one thing customers want with their food, it's evenly cut, aesthetically pleasing grass.

It being a Wednesday, Mrs. Chesterfield had gone to her free tai chi class in the park across town. The Wednesday and Saturday classes always had the best instructor. Tough, but in a nonjudgmental way. Mr. Chesterfield had forgotten all about Mrs. Chesterfield's class, so when Carl finally woke up, he did so in an empty house—and around the time he should have been in second period.

Carl never got ready for school faster than he did that morning. His socks didn't match. His teeth probably could've been brushed longer. His hair was more of a mess than usual. He didn't even have time to process where his parents might be. He only knew he needed to get to school. And quickly.

So he ran. Down the old town house's steps and up the street. Two lefts, and then a right. Feet and arms pumping as quickly as they could carry him until he came to a stop three blocks from school.

When Carl saw the art shop, he knew he needed to dip inside. He had an idea that would require class to wait a few minutes longer.

Carl sprinted toward the school's front door. If he could beat the second bell between third and fourth period, he could seamlessly slip into class with the rest of the stragglers. Yes, luck was on his side as he leaped up the steps into the hall. He'd beaten the bell! He would—

BBBBRRRIIIINNNGGGG—BBBBRRRIIIINNNGGGG

—be twenty seconds too late.

Carl's entrance wasn't as seamless as he had hoped.

As he stood and caught his breath, he heard rustling in what should have been an empty hallway. He looked up to see Bee, who seemed to have lost something in her locker. He gathered his courage and marched up to her as confidently as he could manage.

Carl cleared his throat. Bee pulled her head from the messiest locker in school.

"Hi," he said.

"Hi."

Carl took another deep breath and thought about what to say next. He needed to start planning these things better. Bee looked confused. Then she looked back into her locker. Found whatever she was looking for and put it in her backpack. Carl waited patiently while she zipped the bag shut. Then he continued:

"I, um, got you something."

He reached into his pocket and pulled out a new green metallic marker. Freshly purchased from the art store. It took Bee a beat to realize what it was.

"Oh. You didn't have to do that."

"I, uh, felt like I owed you one." Carl kept holding out the marker. So Bee took it with a smirk.

"Thanks, Carl."

Carl felt a tap on his shoulder and heard a voice behind him.

"You know, my closest friend in the world is a deputy adjutant general in the Pittsburgh (Reserve) National Guard. When he's not on active duty he's the commandant for the city's Soldierly Institute for Misguided Youths."

Carl gulped and then turned into the crossed arms of Principal Wilkinson. The man seemed more disapproving than usual.

"Public school isn't for everyone," continued Wilkinson. "Sometimes military school can get a young man's life back on track. Yours seems headed off the rails. I think Commandant Livermore would be happy to have you aboard. If I expelled you, his institution might be your only option to continue your education. Private school can be awfully expensive, but Livermore gives out scholarships at my recommendation. Some marching might do you good. He's a firm believer that learning to march as a unit can fix just about any problem. The uniforms are a little itchy, but they'll be the least of your concerns."

Carl swallowed hard.

"I'm honestly not a bad guy, Mr. Chesterfield," Wilkinson continued. "You're just going to need to make better decisions, or I'm going to have to call Commandant Livermore so you can complete your education elsewhere."

Carl nodded.

"But for now, both of you go to class," continued Wilkinson. "And Carl, why don't you march to detention after school?"

"Why does only he get detention?" asked Bee.

"Just go to class, Bee."

"But I missed the second bell, too."

Carl gestured for Bee to stay out of it.

"Why don't I have detention?" she persisted.

"Worry about yourself," cautioned the principal.

Carl prayed that Bee would take the advice.

"I don't want special treatment."

Principal Wilkinson shook his head, patted a hand on the back of his neck.

"Especially," Bee said, "from a creep."

"Fine. You both have detention."

———◆———

Detention was in Ms. Turla's Latin classroom. Ms. Turla seemed to be nine hundred years old. She wore clip-on earrings the size of tangerines and the same faded blue dress with an artichoke print every day. The kids used to say she knew Latin because that's what people spoke when she was a little girl. It was an old joke, but not as old as she was. Only a handful of students took her class (the same ones who went to the high school in the morning for advanced math), so Carl had never met the woman.

Carl entered detention to find Ms. Turla slumped over her desk. Asleep? Was she breathing? Wait, was she—

"Sit down and don't talk!" the old teacher barked.

Carl nearly flew from his sneakers. Apparently slumped was how incredibly old teachers sat. He saw Bee drawing in the back and took the seat next to her.

"Howdy, stranger," she said.

"We're not supposed—" mouthed Carl.

"She can't hear us."

Carl looked at the ancient Latin teacher. She remained sprawled over her desk.

"Oh. Uh, sorry again. About getting us in trouble."

"You gotta stop saying that. I'm here because I was late for class. Not because of you."

"Oh."

"What do you think?" she asked as she held up a sketch of a bridge collapsing on Principal Wilkinson. Not limited by the edges of her sketchpad, she had covered her desk in doodles as well: a panda playing an electric guitar, a jet-car jumping over their school, and Carl's personal favorite, Bee's mother surfing on top of a cable car climbing Pittsburgh's Duquesne Incline.

"You, um, have a gift."

"Thank you, Carl."

"Nice to see you, Teddy. Have a seat," cooed Ms. Turla.

Carl was surprised to see his skinny, windbreakered Midnight Brigade associate.

"Ugh, it's you," growled Bee.

Teddy sighed and rolled his eyes as he slid into the chair on the other side of Carl.

"You two know each other?" asked Carl.

"Unfortunately," they both replied.

Carl looked at Teddy and Bee. Searched for a clue to their history. He only picked up the lack of eye contact between them.

"You got detention, too?" asked Carl.

"Of course not. This is where I wait for my father to pick me up."

"No one cares, Teddy."

"Carl asked."

"Whatever."

Carl glanced at Teddy, then Bee again. Odd.

"So what exactly was I supposed to see under that bridge yesterday?" asked Bee.

"You took her to a bridge?"

"I'm talking to Carl, Teddy."

"I am, too." Teddy leaned in conspiratorially. "Anything to report?"

"Report?" laughed Bee. "What is he, your bridge monitor?"

Teddy shrugged. "I suppose that's one way to describe it."

Carl's cheeks went red. Bee and Teddy waited for Carl to explain.

"Well?"

Carl looked from one to the other.

Maybe this was one of those times when it would be best to say as little as possible.

But maybe Teddy and Bee could be trusted? Maybe they didn't count as an "anyone" Frank had asked him not to tell. Perhaps if he embraced his shyness he could maintain Frank's secret. But he didn't want to lie to Teddy and Bee. What to say?

"It's, uh, all fine. Kind of a misunderstanding."

Bee and Teddy stared at Carl. Neither believed him.

"Really," continued Carl.

"But you thought you saw something?" asked Teddy.

Carl took a minute to choose his words carefully. "It wasn't what I, uh, thought."

Bee and Teddy waited for more. It wasn't coming.

Teddy scratched his head. "Listen, I'm sorry if I'm misinterpreting here, Carl, but that kinda sounds like a lie of omission. Like you're choosing your words carefully and you know something that you're not telling us?"

Carl's eyes were twice as big as usual. He wondered if all of his lies of omission had been that obvious. He glanced at Bee. Suddenly, she seemed on the same page as Teddy.

"Sorry to put you on the spot," Teddy continued. "But consider this a safe space. You can say anything."

Carl looked from Teddy to Bee. Swallowed.

"No. I, um, can't."

"Sure you can," said Teddy.

Carl weighed his options. Frowned.

"Really. I can't."

"Fine," they said.

And Teddy folded his arms and glared out the window, and Bee scooted her chair toward the opposite wall and turned to her sketchpad, and Carl dropped his head on his desk, and Ms. Turla began to snore.

"Thanks a lot, Teddy," grumbled Bee.

"Like it's my fault he's not comfortable talking to me in front of you," said Teddy.

Bee shook her head. "You have that so backward. Just like everything else in your life."

Teddy grunted and Bee grunted right back.

Carl lifted his head from the desk. Looked at Bee. Then looked at Teddy. "Why don't, um, you two like each other?"

Teddy and Bee let out aggressive sighs.

"Our parents are dating," they mumbled.

Carl's mouth fell open as Principal Wilkinson peeked into the classroom.

"Ready to go, son?"

CHAPTER TWELVE

P rincipal Wilkinson's bicycle was technically a racing bike, but he never used it for anything close to racing. If he and Teddy pedaled any more slowly down the sidewalk, their bikes would tip over. They just weren't ever in a hurry when they were together. Their rides home through downtown Pittsburgh tended to be the highlights of their days, and they often became so lost in conversation that their handlebars touched.

"Use the bike lane!" screamed the old woman who jumped out of their way.

"Feels dangerous with all the cars!" Wilkinson hollered back.

"Have a great afternoon!" called Teddy, his red hair blowing in the wind as he turned back to his father. "I just don't understand why you don't like him."

"I've spent thirty years identifying troublemakers. I know one when I see one. Carl Chesterfield is not the type of person you should be associating with."

"Bee seems to be friendly with him."

Principal Wilkinson shook his head, reached down, and tucked the cuffs of his khakis farther into his socks. "I think we both know she's going through a rough patch. Her judgment of character isn't as sharp as it should be."

Teddy nodded. He couldn't disagree.

"Get off the sidewalk!" yelled the man stepping out of the restaurant.

"Thanks for your concern!" replied Teddy.

"Look," his father continued, "I'd like you to have friends your own age. I just don't want you to have the wrong friends."

"I don't want to have the wrong friends either."

"Good. I'm not going to forbid you from being polite to the boy. I would just recommend—and this is from my own extensive experience—that you remain extremely cautious and keep your distance."

"I worry that might be an overreaction, Dad."

"You have plenty of other classmates you could socialize with instead."

"That's true in theory, but not in practice."

Wilkinson sighed. "I know it's not the easiest thing in the world being at the same school as me, but—"

"Dad, anyone who doesn't see how great you are isn't worth being friends with in the first place."

Principal Wilkinson smiled. "Thanks. But trust me, that kid

is bad news." Then he swerved to barely avoid colliding with a woman walking her bulldog.

Teddy used the phone in his father's home office for important conversations. And calls to his sister, Veronica, were of the utmost importance. Today's call was also a well-deserved reward for completing two-thirds of his math homework. Teddy sprawled across the office's leather couch while wearing his sneakers.

"It's not that I think Dad is wrong; it's just that I don't think he has all the information," Teddy explained.

"I understand, but do you think it's possible you may not have all the information either?" asked Veronica.

"*That* I'll willingly admit, but I think it's only fair that I proclaim that I am constantly absorbing and seeking out as much knowledge about anything and everything as I can."

"Proclamation noted," she said.

"It's just that Carl strikes me as the kind of person who Dad would appreciate after he got to know him. Only, I need to get to know Carl a little more first. You see, I think Carl is hiding something from me. Not something bad. But definitely not good."

There was a pause on the other end of the phone. "Wait. What?"

"I'm not saying it makes Carl untrustworthy, but I wouldn't say it makes him entirely trustworthy either."

"Hold on. Whose side are you on here—Dad's or Carl's?" asked Veronica.

"Well, my side, of course. But I hear you. I'm not all-knowing and neither is Dad."

"I'm not sure you do hear me, Teddy. I think you should—"

"No, no. I got it. I know exactly what I need to do. You're helpful as ever, Veronica."

"Wait a sec. Can you just—"

"I love you. Dad's calling. We're going to a new burger place down the street for dinner."

"Hold on. I just—"

"Talk to you later!" Teddy happily hung up and ran down the hall to meet his father. The telephone rang as they left the apartment.

CHAPTER THIRTEEN

C leaning up the grass around the picnic tables didn't jump-start new business. At least not in a noticeable way. It was a slow Tuesday. The whole week had been slow.

"Still no repeat customers," sighed Mr. Chesterfield.

Carl gave his father a weak smile from the other side of the food truck. He'd come by to do his homework and provide moral support. The smile didn't help as much as Carl had hoped, but the homework was getting done. His dad had been in a bad mood since he arrived.

"I had a burger returned today," continued Mr. Chesterfield. "Can you believe that? They didn't even want a new one. Just wanted the money back. Some people..."

Carl took a long look at the burger his father had made him for dinner. He poked it with a finger. Rock-hard. And clearly unseasoned. But his father was in the dumps. What could he say?

"I guess not, uh, everyone knows a good thing when they have it."

Mr. Chesterfield snorted. "Right? You said it, kiddo."

The man reached over and ruffled his son's hair. He did that sometimes when Carl did something that cheered him up. It was one of Carl's favorite things.

"I don't know what else I can be doing. I hung more flyers this morning," said Mr. Chesterfield. "Something is up. Did I tell you that huge pile of rocks moved? And I swear there are new scratches on the bridge. A few inches deep, too."

The boy flinched so hard that he lost his pencil.

"Those rocks moved at least seven feet," said Mr. Chesterfield. "I'm sure of it. There was a big patch of grass next to them yesterday, and when I came in this morning to trim things up, the patch was covered by the pile. Three or four tons of stones just moving overnight? Yep, something's up."

Something was up, indeed. Frank had come out from his pile.

And scratches a few inches deep on a steel bridge?

Carl would need to see that troll again.

———◆———

Carl left the old town house slightly after two in the morning. He must have gone to the bridge too early the previous week. It made sense that a troll would wait until the wee hours of the morning to come out. The longer Frank stayed hidden, the less likely it was that he would be seen. That's typically how hiding works.

Carl had unanswered questions about the troll. And questions about what was happening to his city. Thankfully, his shyness didn't extend to bridge-dwelling creatures.

He didn't see a single Pittsburgher on his walk to the food truck. The boy arrived to find the rock pile scattered across the tastefully manicured patches of grass. It took a moment for Carl to spot the silhouette beneath the bridge. Sometimes things can be so big and obvious that you don't see them at first.

As Carl passed the picnic tables, he noticed that a long wooden slat was missing from one of the benches. And as he approached Frank, who sat with his crusty feet dangling into the Ohio River, he saw that the troll was using that slat as a make-shift fishing pole.

The troll sighed and shook his head.

"Had a feeling you'd be back."

Carl smiled and took a seat next to him, surprising himself with how quickly he'd become comfortable with the troll.

"I'm worried about the bridge."

"Hasn't been raided once since I got here."

"Pittsburgh's bridges get raided?"

"Apparently not."

The boy and the troll admired the gorgeous bridge in the moonlight.

"Some of the best bridges in the world are right here in this city," said Frank.

"Yeah?"

"Yeah. And I've been all over. I'm kind of a bridge connoisseur. They're my passion."

Carl nodded. Frank was speaking his language. He'd learned much about bridges over the years listening to his father.

"France, England, Italy, Denmark, Poland? Magnificent, but nothing on Pittsburgh."

The boy smiled as he dreamed about how wonderful it would be to visit those places. He'd been to his grandparents' house outside Youngstown, Ohio (which was lovely), but never outside the United States.

Carl looked up at the troll. "Wait. How did you get to all those countries?"

"Very carefully, kid. Very carefully."

Carl thought for a moment.

"Is it, um, lonely always traveling by yourself?"

"Sometimes. But I'm not always alone. I've been married fifteen times."

"Fifteen?"

"I'm a few centuries old, kid. I've had time." The troll scratched one of his big droopy ears. "What can I say? I'm an expert on love."

"But you've had, uh, fifteen relationships not work out? Does that really make you an expert?"

Frank shrugged.

"I can tell you from experience what doesn't work."

Carl had to admit the troll's logic tracked.

"You married?"

"Not really old enough for that."

"Right. Anyone you have your eye on?"

Carl smiled at nothing in particular. "There's a girl I like."

"What do you like about her?"

"Um." Carl stared at the river, sighed. "Everything. She's smart. Funny. She draws cool pictures. She's, uh, fearless."

The troll nodded.

"What should she like about you?"

Carl's eyes went wide. He was unprepared for the interrogation.

"Well, um, I'm really nice?"

"Is that a question?"

"Uh, no. Statement."

"Nice...Wow. I guess nice is fine. But you're kind of supposed to be nice already. That's just not a negative thing."

Carl frowned as the troll continued.

"All the things you like about her are added value. Things she can use to make the world better. You gotta figure out what you can offer."

"Like what?"

"In my experience, women like guys who live under bridges. There's something appealing about a guy who's self-sufficient like that. A little mysterious. But I don't know, kid, you gotta do you. Just *better* you. Be bold. Or at least entertaining. But bold is best."

Something tugged on Frank's fishing line.

"Ugh. Finally."

Without a reel, Frank whipped the wooden slat over his

shoulder, catapulting a big gooey mess from the water. A nine-pound shovelhead catfish flopped onto the riverbank. The whiskers sprouting from its face were nearly a foot long. Frank let out a heavy sigh.

"More catfish. I hate catfish. Just hate, hate, hate catfish."

Carl eyed the odd-looking fish flopping on the bank, its puffy lips opening and closing. There was nothing appetizing about it.

"I could bring you food tomorrow."

Frank's face lit up (the catfish's face would've, too, if it understood English).

"Really?"

"Um, sure. My dad owns that food truck, remember?"

"Well, how about that..." The troll unhooked the fish and chucked it into the river. "Being bold already."

"And nice?"

"Tomato, tomahto."

"Can I ask you something?"

"Oh boy."

"Why'd you stop protecting bridges?"

Frank held Carl's gaze, then looked to the steel marvel above them. "I wasn't worthy anymore, kid."

"But what if our bridges were in trouble? You'd step in, right?"

Frank swallowed hard. "It doesn't really work like that. I can't—"

"Oh my gosh!" exclaimed Teddy as he emerged from behind the rocks. "So this is what you were hiding. I thought for sure it would be a giant ape or lizard!"

Carl went slack-jawed. As he scrambled to shield Frank with his body, Frank attempted to hide behind his makeshift fishing pole. Neither the pole nor Carl was at all effective in hiding the enormous troll.

"I knew there were monsters," continued Teddy.

"He's not a monster. He's a troll."

"Kinda sounds like you're arguing semantics, Carl."

Frank rubbed a hand on his brow. "You gotta be kidding me, kid. I ask one favor . . ."

"He talks?" Teddy exclaimed. "So he's the one that's been attacking our bridges?"

"He's hasn't—"

"I mean, come on!" said Frank. "How hard is it to not tell anyone? You just have to do *nothing*."

"But I didn't. This is my friend, Teddy."

"I don't care who it is, kid. We had an understanding."

"But Teddy's into defending bridges."

"Oh, he is?" Frank asked facetiously. "Great! I was just thinking Pittsburgh could use a scrawny human kid to defend its bridges!"

"That was rude," mumbled Teddy.

"I'm sorry," said Carl. "But if you, um, just—"

"Whoa!" exhaled Bee as she stumbled from the other side of the rocks. Her face dropped when she saw Teddy. "Ugh. You're here, too?"

"Evening, Bee."

Frank threw his hands in the air. "How many people did you tell about me, kid?"

"Zero! Well, um, no one directly?"

"*Directly?*"

"Maybe I, uh, said some things to a couple of people that made them suspicious and caused them to investigate?"

"Cool troll," said Bee.

"Well, her I like," conceded Frank.

Carl nodded, then smiled toward Bee. His gaze lingered. Frank calmed down a little and smirked at the boy, pieces seemingly clicking into place for the troll.

"Is he here to protect the bridge?" asked Bee.

"He doesn't do that anymore."

"Why not?"

"We were just, um, getting to that."

"No we weren't," said Frank.

"So, you're a troll who *doesn't* protect bridges?" asked Bee.

"Who *used to* protect bridges," corrected Frank.

"But now you destroy them?" questioned Teddy.

Frank covered his face with his hands and shook his head. "Help me out here, kid?"

"This is Frank," explained Carl. "He, um, just lives under this bridge."

"I suppose Frank's a good enough name for a troll," said Teddy.

"That's what I said!"

"I feel like I'm in a nightmare that keeps repeating," muttered Frank.

"Why don't you protect bridges anymore?" asked Bee.

"Things happen. Trolls change."

"You mean you quit? Doesn't feel right for a troll to just give up protecting bridges," said Teddy.

"Have you met a lot of trolls?"

"No. But still seems fishy. Have you guys seen these scratches over here?"

"Things aren't always as bad as they seem," said Frank.

"Why would a troll live under a bridge if he wasn't going to protect it?" said Teddy.

"It's my natural habitat," said Frank.

"Can you teach us how to defend bridges?" asked Bee.

"Not really something I can tell you how to do in a night."

"Well, um, what can you tell us tonight?" asked Carl.

"That it's time for you and your friends to go, but if you bring me that food tomorrow I'll let you come back."

Teddy groaned. "But we have so many questions for you!"

"But I have so little patience for *you*."

"Agreed," mumbled Bee.

"What is this? Burlap?" Teddy asked, tugging at Frank's tunic.

"It's leather," grumbled Frank.

"Must be really old leather."

Frank sighed. "Seriously, bedtime. Everyone get out of here so I can wallow in past mistakes and regrets. And, kid..." The troll paused and locked eyes with Carl. "Remember—*be bold*."

CHAPTER FOURTEEN

t took all of Bee's energy to not scream at Teddy on the walk home from the bridge.

Teddy wouldn't stop talking about how brilliant and correct he had been and how he thought something was off about Frank. Bee nodded and offered things like "Uh-huh," "Yep," and "That's so fascinating, Teddy" as he rambled through his theories about what was happening to the bridges. They all had to do with different kinds of monsters. Monsters he'd seen on television. A few he'd read about in comic books. Even some he'd dreamt up on his own. And now knowing that trolls were real made Teddy believe his theories were much more possible, likely even. It was ridiculous and drove Bee insane. She would normally be the last person to avoid a fight, but she didn't want to ruin an amazing night with an argument.

Just before she turned down her street, she realized that Carl hadn't said a word since they left the bridge. She glanced his way to find him staring off at the city and smiling. It made her smile, too. Then they all said their good-nights.

Bee thought about that smile again after class the following day as she sat on the school's front steps to draw and clear her head. Something had changed with Carl. Something she couldn't place. It wasn't that he was taller. But maybe his posture was better?

Bee liked being a loner at school. She avoided other kids by choice—didn't mind that many saw her as intimidating. But lately, spending time with Carl hadn't exactly been awful. She even found herself looking forward to seeing him, especially since she was becoming a loner at home as well. Then, like magic, she looked up and saw him leaving the building.

"Hi, Carl."

She watched his face squish together like he was trying to think of something funny, clever, or confident to say. It was the same expression a person would make upon feeling the initial signs of an upset stomach. Maybe Carl hadn't changed after all. She turned back to her sketch. But as she drew a fog of feelings and concerns swelled inside her, followed by an overwhelming desire to let them out.

"He went out with my mom again last night," she said without looking up. "That's every night this week. Can you believe it?"

Carl took a bold-ish seat next to her.

"She's been lonely since my dad left," she continued as she shaded her sketch. "She says she doesn't have anyone to talk to, and for some reason she can talk to him. I told her she could talk to me, but she says it's not the same. It used to be us going out three or four nights a week, discovering new foods, meeting people we wouldn't normally meet. Just me and her. But now it's more her and Wilkinson, and I get left with some overworked intern from the newspaper trying to score points with my mom by babysitting."

Carl nodded. She got the sense that he understood what she was saying. Or at least that he wanted to.

"They met when she got called to his office because I had too many tardies," Bee whispered. "And I had too many tardies because I was always out late with her. Can you believe that?" Bee exhaled. "Well, at least it's Wednesday. Review Night is always the best night of the week. We get dressed up and go out to a new restaurant, and we talk about anything except the food, because when we get home we each write our own reviews of dinner and then switch. They usually end up being pretty close. I guess I got my taste buds from her." Bee tapped her fingernails together. "Lately I don't know what she's thinking."

She wondered if he would say something about his own parents. Wondered if he ever had sleepless nights worrying about all the things in the world that couldn't be controlled. Wondered if his parents fought like hers used to before they split. It looked like he wanted to share something. But all that came out was:

"I keep, uh, worrying Principal Wilkinson will get me sent to military school."

"He does mention his best friend a lot," said Bee. "The deputy adjutant general in the Pittsburgh (Reserve) National Guard... Like it'll impress me or something."

Bee and Carl watched a school bus pull away from the parking lot. They took in the neighborhood for a moment. Neither made eye contact with the other.

"Sometimes I wish I could just sit my parents down and explain to them how the world works," she continued.

"I, um, know what you mean."

She smiled.

"That was fun last night. You might be a little more interesting than I thought. You don't have to be so invisible, Carl."

She watched his cheeks heat up. Then she smirked as he struggled to find something to say. Not wanting him to squirm too much, she asked:

"Can I ask you something?"

"Sure."

"And I don't mean to hurt your feelings."

Carl swallowed hard. Like he was bracing for impact.

"Okay..."

"What's wrong with your hair?" she said with a laugh.

Carl chuckled.

"My, uh, mom cuts it."

"Ah."

She placed her baseball cap on his head. "Better," she said.

Because it was. He wore her cap for the rest of the school year.

"And take this, too," she said as she tore her drawing from the sketchpad. "Thanks for being cool about us butting in on your secret."

She'd drawn a perfect likeness of Frank sitting under the bridge. His knees hugged to his chest. Her signature in a corner.

The troll looked sad.

A crystal chandelier hung in the middle of the dining room, and the servers wore crisp white smocks. That kind of uniform always made Bee nervous. How did they keep them so clean? She figured their dry-cleaning bills were astronomical.

The restaurant they'd chosen for Review Night was called Paris in Spring. She found the name equal parts pleasant and generic, which was also what she thought of the appetizers. Bee had a hunch that her mother felt the same way, but she wouldn't know for sure until they exchanged reviews later that evening. Her mother's editor had pestered her to review the place for months. Apparently she had gone to college with the owner. That kind of thing always ended poorly. Favor reviews were never as glowing as the editor wanted, and the food was never as delicious as Maddy Lee wanted.

"I hope you enjoy," the server said as he delivered their entrees. "The chef uses a secret ingredient that makes his chicken one of a kind."

Bee took a whiff of the dish as the server departed. "Truffle salt?"

Maddy Lee winked at her daughter.

Bee smiled and made a note to herself on her little pad on the table. "Why does everyone think that's a secret ingredient? I mean, I like it and all, but secret? It has such a distinct taste and smell. It's like truffle salt is half of all secret ingredients these days. Who do they think they're fooling?"

Maddy smiled.

"Sorry, we should wait until we read each other's reviews to talk about this," Bee said. "I saw this gourmet corn dog place by the ballpark that I thought we could try tomorrow night."

"That sounds fun, but tomorrow's not possible."

Bee smirked as she thought of Frank living under the bridge downtown. "I've recently decided that nothing is impossible."

"Oh yeah?" Maddy asked with a raise of her brow.

Bee eyed her mother and debated how much she could say and how she could say it. "Have you ever come across anything truly incredible in this city? Like, something you didn't think could be that was? Maybe when you were chasing a story for work?"

Maddy thought for a moment. "Well, once I was working on a piece about a new steakhouse, and its kitchen literally had three dozen different kinds of health code violations."

Bee shook her head. "No. That's not what I mean. I mean something that's supposed to be *impossible*. Like, actually amazing. Otherworldly, even."

Maddy bit her lip; then her face lit up. "I know! Last year I had to cover one of those competitive eating contests, and some guy from Willow Crest ate seven pounds of chipped chopped ham."

Bee forced a smile. Clearly she and her mother were on different wavelengths. "Right. That's amazing," she said with a nod, deciding to let it go. Then she grimaced. "Wait, why can't we go to dinner tomorrow night?"

"I'm going out with Barry."

"Who?"

"Principal Wilkinson?"

"Oh."

"Maybe we can go next week?"

"Feels like you're going out with him a lot."

"I like him, Bee."

Bee poked her chicken with her fork. "Do you have to?"

"I do." Maddy smiled. "Trust me. He's a good one. What do you think about the three of us going to that corn dog place together?"

Bee closed her notepad and frowned at the chandelier.

"I honestly can't think of anything worse."

CHAPTER FIFTEEN

C arl felt good about his talk with Bee in front of the school. He was gaining confidence and knew it was at least in part due to her. Bee was bold. She hadn't thought twice about meeting Frank under the bridge. She'd simply accepted the information, then confidently moved forward. It was a quality that Carl admired in her and wished he had more of himself. How could he become bold, too?

Soon Carl realized that simply wanting to be bolder made him *feel* bolder. So perhaps he was? Plus, being able to share his secret was a weight off his back. With one less thing holding him down, Carl Chesterfield was practically floating through Pittsburgh. Now he just needed to figure out how to get the troll fed.

He didn't know how many hamburgers Frank could eat but was certain he wouldn't be able to bring enough to test the troll's limits. Before he'd left for school that morning he'd told his mother he would bring food home. That afternoon at the truck, he told his father that he and his mother wanted to have burgers for dinner and that they should have extras at the house in case anyone got hungry. Another lie of omission, Carl supposed, since he had a very specific, incredibly hungry "anyone" in mind.

"Do you think six hamburgers is enough?" asked Mr. Chesterfield.

"I was, uh, thinking a dozen."

Mr. Chesterfield shrugged and fired up the grill. "Guess I have time and burgers to spare. You know, you're still my only repeat customer. I wish you were paying, but I have to admit, I'm thrilled that you want more."

"Thanks, Dad."

Mr. Chesterfield began slapping hamburger patties down; each sizzled and fired off steam as it hit the grill. "Business has been trickling off instead of growing. I spent most of the day wondering if I used the wrong color paper for my flyers."

"Oh. Maybe?"

"That's what I'm thinking. Maybe I should have used red? An eye-catcher? Or yellow? Like a taxi? I think I read somewhere that taxis are yellow because it's the easiest color to spot. It was either that or yellow is the cheapest color of paint."

Carl nodded. "Did you do anything else today?"

"Honestly? I found some of our old laminated menus and used them like a deck of cards to build a pyramid on one of the picnic tables."

"You did?"

"I did. And I got it six stories tall before I couldn't reach any higher."

"Wow."

"Yep. I was thinking that if I had you on my shoulders we could add another two stories."

Carl smiled and shook his head at his father.

After the twelve patties were cooked, they were wrapped in aluminum foil (for easy reheating) and placed in a canvas bag along with a dozen hamburger buns. Then Carl and his father used the old laminated menus to build a pyramid on one of the empty picnic tables. Mr. Chesterfield put Carl on his shoulders after they built the sixth story, and the two were able to add three stories more before the menus collapsed. After that, they lined up the three picnic tables and used the menus to make a bridge that ran across them.

Carl and his father hadn't built a bridge together in years. They used to construct them all the time when Carl was little. Back then, they used pipe cleaners, paper towels, pillows, clothes hangers, once even shoe boxes and shoes, but this was the first time they'd used menus. They worked well. And it felt good to build together again.

When they finished, they stood back to admire their work. Mr. Chesterfield hung an arm on Carl's shoulder. "I used to daydream about making bridges when I was your age. I'd sneak into Grandpa's office and flip through his old blueprints and latest designs. I couldn't wait to design my own."

"So you always knew what you wanted?" asked Carl.

"Always knew, but when I finally got to engineering school, I almost flunked out my freshman year. There was so much more math than I expected! My professors suggested I switch to a less demanding major at a less challenging college. But Grandpa and Grandma had already sacrificed so much and spent so much money. I just couldn't imagine letting them down and not succeeding. So I got a tutor, and I basically studied around the clock until I graduated. I had to work harder than everyone else because it didn't come as naturally to me, but by the time I finished I was number one in my class."

Carl smiled at his father.

"I don't give up easily, Carl. Especially when family is involved."

Then Mr. Chesterfield gave his son a pat on the back and Carl walked the canvas bag home, knowing full well that he would be walking ten of those patties back later that evening.

The patties were placed in the refrigerator, and Bee's sketch of Frank was taped to the wall across from Carl's bed. He stared at Bee's signature before pulling his journal from beneath the mattress to write:

> But inside she worried she was being forgotten.
> Replaced by her principal, which felt rather rotten.

———◆———

Mrs. Chesterfield had fallen into the habit of rushing out of her dental office the moment the clock struck five. What had once been her dream job was now just work, and she often counted the seconds until she could return home. She didn't remember constantly feeling this tired, and as each day passed she was more drained than the last.

With Carl and Mr. Chesterfield out of the house more and more, there were fewer and fewer things for her to do outside the office. And when Carl had announced that he would bring dinner home that evening, there was one less. So Mrs. Chesterfield sat and waited in the old town house.

When Carl arrived, he took the liberty of heating two of the twelve patties on the stove, and then placed the patties between a pair of buns. All the while, Mrs. Chesterfield sat at the oak island appreciating her son's independence. As Mrs. Chesterfield bit into her dinner, she got the sense that something was missing. And not just seasoning from her average hamburger. Mrs. Chesterfield missed being motivated. Missed being passionate. Missed being surprised and excited. Her life desperately needed a spark. She needed something wonderful.

CHAPTER SIXTEEN

C arl crept into the kitchen at a quarter to three. He quietly lit the stove and reheated the remaining patties, then rewrapped them in foil. He placed the burgers and buns in the canvas tote and snuck out of the old town house.

Sneaking out to the bridge was becoming routine. Pittsburgh was so calm and quiet at this time of night that it felt like a different city. One that belonged entirely to Carl if only for a little while. No honking, shouting, music, or foot traffic. Just Carl and Pittsburgh.

He smiled as he cut through Point State Park, thirty-six gorgeous acres in the middle of downtown Pittsburgh. He beamed with pride as he thought of the city's incredible sports teams, unmatched collections of dinosaur bones, and contributions to the worlds of painting and sculpting. He marveled at the resourcefulness of whoever had thought to turn all those old steel factories into beautiful lofts and museums.

Carl closed his eyes and began to feel light-headed as he pictured his favorite views of the city from the top of Mount Washington. He opened his eyes as he walked by a series of Andy Warhol–esque posters (featuring bridges made of soup cans) advertising City Celebration. He couldn't believe it was less than three weeks away. Goose bumps sprouted up and down his arms. It was like Pittsburgh was confirming he was exactly where he should be. He wondered if the parade committee had gotten his letter.

As Carl passed the red awning, Bee and Teddy strode out and fell into step on either side of him. The Midnight Brigade was now three members strong and about to embark on its most important mission yet.

———◆———

Frank paced beneath the bridge's near tower. The kids smiled and hustled the last fifty or so yards to the troll, delighted to see their monstrous friend. Frank looked stressed. He rubbed his belly and let out a sigh of relief when he saw Carl holding the bag.

"Was starting to think you weren't coming, kid."

"We, um brought the burgers."

"Good, good. I almost started fishing."

Carl kneeled before the troll and slipped burgers between buns. Frank leaned over him and smacked his lips.

"If I had to eat one more catfish from that river . . . Honestly, I don't know what I'd do, kid. You're a lifesaver."

Teddy looked up at the troll. "I still don't know how I feel about you."

Frank nodded. "I appreciate your honesty."

"Don't mind him," said Bee. "He's burdened with bad genes."

"Must be rough."

Bee shrugged. "Not as rough as being abandoned by your mother for those bad genes."

"He's a great guy once you get to know him," explained Teddy.

Frank looked at Bee. Seemed to sense how troubled she was. "Everyone leaves at some point or another. It's whether they come back that sets them apart. I wouldn't sweat it."

"I'm not so sure," said Bee.

"Just wait."

Bee smiled. "You're a good troll, Frank. I wish my mom could find someone like you."

Teddy shook his head as he strolled away to get a closer look at the bridge. Bee stepped up to get a closer look at Frank.

"You're not as gigantic as I remember," she said.

"Thanks."

"It looks like this bridge has fresh scratches," called Teddy.

"Don't worry yourself," responded the troll.

"This one's six inches deep," continued Teddy.

"That steel is three feet thick." Frank looked at the burgers. Frowned. "You got any ketchup or mustard?"

Carl finished assembling the burgers. Sighed.

"Come on, Carl," groaned Bee.

"I forgot. But that's not really how my dad makes them anyway. He, uh, serves 'em plain."

"Isn't this city known for its toppings?" asked Frank.

"Among other things."

"But your dad..."

"Makes 'em plain."

"Right."

"I've been trying to teach Carl," explained Bee.

"She has," he confirmed.

Frank shook his head. Took in his well-done dinner a moment longer. Gave it a sniff, then scooped up the burgers in one hand and shoveled them into his mouth. Carl and Bee watched expectantly. Frank's face soured the more he chewed.

"Hmmpf," Frank said through bites.

"Are they, um, good?" Carl asked, hoping trolls had more forgiving taste buds than people.

Frank swallowed. It seemed difficult to do so. He held up a finger, asking for a moment. Then he walked to the riverbank, got down on his belly, and took a nice long drink from the Ohio River. The troll wiped his mouth and returned.

"Well, they're not *bad* per se."

Carl did his best to stand tall and take the criticism. Bee gave Carl a supportive pat on the back.

"It's just that they're kind of . . . average?" said Frank.

Carl glowed.

"Thank you!"

"Thank you?"

"Well, um, yeah. That was my dad's goal. Average food for the average customer."

Bee and the troll grimaced. Frank took a beat to choose his words carefully. "Kid, nobody wants average food."

Carl turned to Bee to find her awkwardly examining Mr. Chesterfield's freshly cut grass.

"Oh." Carl nodded. It made so much sense coming from the troll. And seemed in line with what Bee had been telling him.

"And listen, don't get me wrong, it's not that I'm not appreciative. It's just that—" Frank opened and closed his mouth a few times. Rolled his jaw. "It's just that, ya know, good is good."

"Hard to argue with that," said Bee.

"Not trying to be harsh, kid," Frank said.

"No. I get it," said Carl.

"Great. I want to make sure we're okay." Frank gestured back and forth between them. Then the troll popped his mouth open and shut again. He looked like the catfish from the previous night.

"Uh, totally."

"Good, good. So, just to ask, how's the other food in your dad's truck?"

"Average." Carl chuckled.

"Figur—" Frank reached into his mouth and started tapping one of his molars. "Ugh. Ow. This again."

"Are you all right?"

The troll shook his head and rubbed his jaw. "Just something I've been dealing with. Usually acts up when I eat."

"Is it painful?" asked Bee.

"It's not great."

"Is there, uh, anything you can do to make the pain go away?"

Frank glanced at the bridge. Let his shoulders slump.

"Look, this is kinda embarrassing. And it's not gonna sound terrific. Just—well, never mind."

"Just what?" asked Teddy, strolling back from the bridge.

"It's just—" Frank caressed his jaw. Peeked at the bridge again. Sighed. "It's just, if I rub my back teeth against something for a bit it makes the pain go away..."

The kids looked from Frank to the scratched suspension bridge.

"Something like a bridge?"

Frank shook his head. "I know how bad it sounds."

Carl threw his hands to Bee's baseball cap on his head as he realized it was Frank who'd caused the bridge to shake all those nights ago. Bee closed her eyes. And Teddy yelled as loudly as he could, "I knew you were the one who was eating our bridges!"

"Whoa! 'Eating our bridges'? That sounds way worse than what I'm doing. I just gnaw on them a little until my tooth stops hurting. I'm not proud of it . . . and I wouldn't do anything to jeopardize a bridge's structural integrity. I mean, I wouldn't do anything to make a bridge fall down."

"We know what jeopardizing structural integrity means," said Bee.

"Oh. Good. I mean, they might move a little when I chew. But nothing serious."

Teddy began to pace. Bee and Carl twiddled their thumbs.

"You don't seem convinced," observed Frank.

"No. We, uh, believe you," said Carl.

"But?"

Carl looked at Bee. The revelation seemed to eat away at her, too. "But didn't you, uh, spend most of your life protecting bridges?"

"I understand the irony, kid. And it's not like I don't feel awful about it. But I don't have any other options."

Carl scratched his head.

"I think I might have one for you."

CHAPTER SEVENTEEN

Mr. Chesterfield snored. Every night. Every nap. Like congested and jarring clockwork. He was Mrs. Chesterfield's personal white noise machine.

Carl stood over his parents' bed and gently shook his mother awake, then put one finger to his lips and another to hers. Nine times out of ten Mrs. Chesterfield would've screamed, being woken up like that, but on this night, she wiped the sleep from her eyes and smiled at her son. The boy pantomimed for her to get dressed and follow him but not to wake his father. Mrs. Chesterfield nodded. She knew she was about to share a secret with Carl.

She threw on warm clothes and followed him out of the room. Mr. Chesterfield's snoring remained constant. When they reached the cozy kitchen, Mrs. Chesterfield put a hand on Carl's shoulder and whispered, "What is it?"

"It's, um, better if I show you," he whispered back.

Mrs. Chesterfield nodded. She trusted her son.

"But before we go," he continued, "do you have an extra set of dental tools?"

Carl and his mother walked in silence toward the bridge. She carried a leather dental bag, the one her parents had bought her after she passed her clinical and written exams. The bag she'd used during the time she felt she had the greatest job in the world. It had been tucked away and forgotten in the back of a closet for years.

Mrs. Chesterfield had a smirk on her face the entire walk over, like she knew something special was about to happen. She could feel it in the cool air. Carl knew it, too. His mother had always been the most dependable person in his life. If anyone he knew could help Frank, it would be her. They would have to work quickly, thought Carl. Early commuters would be on the road in less than an hour. As they grew close, Mrs. Chesterfield seemed confused. Disappointed, even.

"Why did you take me to your father's food truck?"

"It's not the truck," said Carl.

Mrs. Chesterfield spotted Bee sitting on the grass and Teddy pacing. "Who are they?"

"My friends," said Carl. "Don't worry." Then he called toward the near tower supporting the bridge, "It's okay!"

When Frank stepped from behind the tower, Mrs. Chesterfield's bag slipped from her fingers. And she smiled the second-biggest smile of her life (the biggest being the first time she had held her son).

"See, Carl?" she said. "Wonderful things."

———————◆———————

The shock of seeing a giant troll was overridden by Carl's mother's training as a dental hygienist. There was no time for nervousness or unprofessionalism. She had a patient in need.

The troll lounged on his back, mouth opened wide. Mrs. Chesterfield leaned in to get a better look, her head and torso trustingly between the giant's chompers and her hands covered in blue latex gloves. It was difficult to see in the shadow of the bridge, but thankfully, Mrs. Chesterfield knew exactly what she was looking for.

She frowned. Stepped back from the troll.

"It'll have to come out," she said.

"Ugh. I knew it. Will it hurt?" asked the troll.

Mrs. Chesterfield gave Frank a pat on the shoulder.

"I have a hunch you've dealt with worse."

"Doesn't mean I like it ..."

"I'm surprised it hasn't fallen out on its own."

"Are you a licensed dental technician?" asked Teddy.

"Not sure anyone's properly trained for this, but I'll do my best."

"That's reassuring," said Frank.

"You'll probably be fine," said Mrs. Chesterfield before turning to her son, who held her bag at the ready. She opened the bag, did some digging, and pulled out a long syringe.

"I can numb the pain. But I'm not sure how much numbing I can do on someone your size."

"Whoa. Easy...I'm a little sensitive about my weight." Frank's eyes went wide when he saw what she was holding. "Hey! You didn't say anything about needles."

"Don't be a baby."

Mrs. Chesterfield stuck the needle into Frank's gums, injecting them with Novocain. His eyes twitched and he began to drool.

"Amazing!" exclaimed Bee.

"Isn't it? I can't imagine that'll last too long. I certainly don't have pliers that are big enough for this. We're gonna have to do it the old-fashioned way."

Mrs. Chesterfield dipped back into the troll's mouth, put two hands around a green, shoe box–sized molar in a row of yellowish teeth, and tugged as hard as she could. The tooth didn't budge.

"Carl, grab on to me and pull."

"Um, excuse me?" asked Carl.

"Just pull."

Carl put his hands around his mother's waist. She leaned back into the troll's mouth, dragging Carl along with her. The inside of Frank's mouth was warm and sticky. It reminded Carl of a dreadful road trip he'd taken the previous July during which he was cramped in the backseat of his aunt Kelly's sedan with his four older cousins and no air-conditioning. The only thing worse than the mouth's humidity was the smell. It became immediately clear that trolls don't brush their teeth. Frank's mouth reeked like spoiled goat milk and rotten catfish. Or four sweaty older cousins.

Carl began to gag. He held his breath as he held his mother.

"Iss thiss gggonnna—" slurred Frank, careful not to bite down on the woman and her son.

"Pull!" yelled Mrs. Chesterfield.

Carl pulled Mrs. Chesterfield.

Mrs. Chesterfield pulled the tooth.

They strained. Gave it their all.

But the tooth stayed put.

"Aaaaaaah!" moaned Frank.

Mrs. Chesterfield and Carl stepped back from the troll's mouth.

"I donn't thinkk it'sss gonna come out," said Frank.

Mrs. Chesterfield looked at Bee and Teddy. "That Novocain is wearing off already. We're all going to have to work together."

"Are you sure we should be doing this?" whispered Teddy.

"We can trust him, Teddy," said Carl. "He needs our help."

"It doesn't feel right," continued Teddy.

"He's our friend."

"Okay, but don't say I didn't warn you." Teddy shot an uneasy glance at Frank. "I don't have to touch anything repulsive, do I? Because if I don't have to, I'd rather not."

"And I don't want him to touch me," said Bee, gesturing to Teddy with a tilt of her head.

"Like I'd want *you* to touch *me*," scoffed Teddy.

"I'll grab the tooth," announced Mrs. Chesterfield before pointing to Teddy. "You grab me. Carl can grab you."

The kids nodded. Mrs. Chesterfield moved back into Frank's mouth and grabbed the tooth with the tightest grip she could manage. Teddy stepped up and put his hands around Mrs. Chesterfield's waist. Carl grabbed Teddy, took a deep breath, and prepared to pull. Then Carl's knees went weak as he felt Bee's hands reach around and grab him below his arms.

"On three," said Mrs. Chesterfield. "As hard as you can."

"One."

Carl got his head back in the game. Grabbed Teddy tighter. Focused on the task at hand.

"Two! With all your might!"

Frank pinched his eyes shut.

"THREE!"

Bee pulled Carl.

And Carl pulled Teddy.

And Teddy pulled Mrs. Chesterfield.

And Mrs. Chesterfield pulled on the tooth (and they all held their breath to avoid the smell).

They tugged and yanked and heaved and jerked as hard as they could, arms and backs straining until . . . the tooth came free!

"Ow!" yelped the troll, as mother, son, and friends fell to the patchy manicured lawn, molar in Mrs. Chesterfield's hands.

Teddy looked at the rotten tooth. Dry-heaved.

Frank rolled his jaw. Staggered to his feet. Wiped some drool.

"That a—that a—" He popped his mouth open and shut. "That feels better already."

"It'll be a little sore for a while," warned Mrs. Chesterfield.

"Whatever. This is unbelievable! You can't imagine how long I've dealt with that. You're magnificent!"

She blushed. "Well, it's just what I do."

Frank grabbed the tooth and inspected it before tossing it into the river.

"Just what you do? Helping people like this every day? You're an angel!"

And it was then that Mrs. Chesterfield felt whatever was missing from her job slide back into place. She shrugged and smiled.

Frank crouched down and gave her the gentlest hug a troll had ever given.

Carl beamed at his mother. She'd saved the day.

CHAPTER EIGHTEEN

T he next morning, Mrs. Chesterfield practically skipped to work. Her smile was so wide that patients could see it through her surgical mask. She spent the day cleaning teeth and asking people if they had been flossing. She stayed at the office until 5:23, caught up in a colleague's exhilarating report about the test results of a new line of toothbrushes. When she came home she was more relaxed than she'd been in years and couldn't wait to tell Carl about her day over dinner. The spark that had gone missing was back. It was one of the most enjoyable Thursdays of her life.

Meanwhile, Mr. Chesterfield had spent his day debating whether he should grow his mustache into a goatee (he decided against it). When Mrs. Chesterfield saw Carl after work, she gave him a wink but made no mention of the troll living under the bridge. She was exceptional at keeping secrets. Carl loved seeing his mother happy. He was thrilled that she'd rediscovered her passion for teeth.

Mr. and Mrs. Chesterfield didn't fight that evening. Nor the night after. Unfortunately, that didn't mean their problems went away. Quite the opposite.

It didn't take Carl's parents long to realize that they weren't bringing in enough money to cover the payments they owed the bank. If Mr. Chesterfield hadn't borrowed so much money for the food truck and the overpriced piece of land, the family could have squeezed by on Mrs. Chesterfield's salary alone. But the interest and mortgage payments had spiraled out of control. Worse still, the family was losing money every day the truck was open. They would be better off if the truck closed and Mr. Chesterfield did nothing at all. The realization devastated them.

Without enough money to pay their bills, there wasn't much Mr. and Mrs. Chesterfield could do other than organize them. At first, they arranged their bills by due date. Then they sorted them by the amount owed. Next they grouped them by the number of notices they had received. Eventually they organized them alphabetically. No matter how they looked at them, it appeared they owed quite a bit. And as each day passed, that quite a bit grew. And with it, their anxiety about what to do.

Mrs. Chesterfield knew how much joy her own job brought her. And she respected her husband's desire to be noble. But maintaining a roof over the family's heads was important, too. Mr. and Mrs. Chesterfield had long nightly talks about the food truck. She was convinced it was unsustainable. He was convinced they were one lucky break away from profitability. She wanted to be supportive, but she also wished he'd be realistic. He wanted to be successful, but he also believed it would magically happen overnight.

It took Carl nearly two weeks to figure out what was going on. Normally his parents yelled at each other, which made listening through the walls a breeze. But calm, considerate discussions made eavesdropping much more difficult. When Carl finally connected the dots, he felt awful for his parents, concerned for his family, and worried about their home. Where would they live? What could they do?

He needed to take his mind off things, so he hopped on his computer and pulled up the City Celebration website. He was thrilled to find that the parade route had been set. But as he zoomed in on the map, his shoulders slumped and his chest felt heavy.

The parade would start on the Hallock Street Suspension Bridge. Just seven city blocks from his father's food truck—but seven city blocks closer to the residential parts of the city. Someone would have to get utterly lost to pass their truck on the way to the parade. The route might as well start in California. His father was right. It was hopeless to think that City Celebration would boost their business. Everything was hopeless.

Carl powered down his computer, climbed into bed, and

counted the rotations of his ceiling fan while he prayed for sleep. He lost count somewhere in the mid–nine thousands and started over. Sleep had become a pipe dream. His worry continued to grow. He eyed Bee's drawing taped to his wall, then snuck out to visit his bridge-dwelling friend.

———————◆———————

"I still can't get the taste out of my mouth," complained Frank.

"The Novocain?" asked Carl.

"The hamburger."

"Oh."

"I've been eating mud and grass all week. Nothing works."

"Yuck."

"You're telling me, kid."

Frank leaned against the bridge. Swirled his tongue around the inside of his mouth. Swallowed. Shook his head. The taste was still there.

Carl walked around the picnic tables, picking up trash. Business being slow, there wasn't much. Only a few hamburger wrappers. A crescent moon shimmered in the sky.

"I can't believe people buy those things from your father."

"Well, uh, most people don't."

"Not doing so well?"

"Nope," sighed Carl as he dumped the wrappers in the trash can. The weight of his father's food truck was on his back. The troll watched Carl for a moment. Saw that the kid looked out of sorts. Antsy.

"Hey, are you okay?"

Carl stared at the Ohio River, lost in thought. "Um, what? Sorry."

Frank exhaled. Took two steps forward and sat cross-legged. Did his best to get to Carl's level.

"You're really worried about your dad, aren't you?"

Carl sighed. "More than usual."

"Right. Well, I've been chewing on that. I think your dad needs to do something to set his food apart. Something bold."

The troll was big on being bold. Carl remained intrigued by the notion.

"Bee had me thinking the same thing. But what?"

"Well, I've been chewing on that, too." Frank smiled. Then he stuck a hand under his tunic and felt around his midsection. His hand emerged with an orange glob of mousse about the size of a softball. It smelled delicious. He extended it to Carl.

"Here. Take it."

Carl took an uneasy look at the goo on Frank's finger. It

reminded him of the gunk that built up behind the family's refrigerator. They cleaned behind it once a year, and last year Carl had the honor of doing the dirty work.

"What do you, uh, want me to do with that?"

"Put it in your hat. It washes right out."

Carl frowned. It felt suspect, but the troll hadn't led him astray yet. He took off Bee's baseball cap, turned it upside down, and allowed Frank to plop the mousse in.

"Well, um, what is this?"

"Just taste it."

"But, uh, wh—"

"Try it. But just a smidge. It's strong."

Carl took another whiff. It did smell wonderful. Sweet and savory at the same time, like cinnamon and cheese. So he took a pinch and dropped it on his tongue. His face lit up.

"Not bad, right?" asked Frank.

"Incredible."

"Yeah. It's a special troll spice. It even makes catfish tolerable. Not good. Tolerable. But again, I hate catfish."

Carl smacked his lips together. "Wow. The, um, aftertaste is even better."

"Yep. Clears your sinuses up, too. Great for cold season."

"Amazing."

"Could definitely improve those burgers. Although I'm not sure burgers are the way to go."

"They're not?"

"Everyone makes hamburgers. Your dad should do something less ordinary. And use the stuff in your hat."

"Less ordinary?"

"Yeah, kid. Aren't you listening? Be better than average. Give people something unexpectedly great. That's what people want in life. And not just from their food."

Carl shoveled a bigger pinch of the goo into his mouth.

"So, this is like a topping?"

"Not like. Is."

"Probably great on toast," mumbled Carl.

"What?"

"Never mind."

Carl took a larger bite of the goo.

"So, what is this?" he asked between chews.

"Belly button lint."

Carl's eyes went wide. Then he spit until he couldn't spit anymore and proceeded to wipe his tongue on the back of his sleeve.

"You're so dramatic, kid. I knew you wouldn't try it if I told you."

"That's disgusting! What's wrong with you?"

Frank shrugged and shook his head. "Take it easy. It's not human belly button lint. It's troll belly button lint. That's a delicacy."

"It's gross!"

"You had seconds and thirds. Did you or did you not think it was fantastic half a minute ago?"

Surprised, Carl took a beat and regained his composure. When he was seven, his grandparents had taken him to a French restaurant where he ate escargot and loved it. He went through an entire loaf of bread dipping it into the garlicky sauce, soaking up and eating every drop of the dish. It wasn't until months later that he learned that escargots were snails. At that point they were safely out of his body. He felt betrayed at first, but in the grand scheme of things he was fine. And he would order the snails again. Maybe this was the same thing.

"I mean, I guess I liked it."

"You loved it. And it's all natural. High in fiber. Trust me, that's nowhere near the grossest thing you've eaten today."

Carl nodded. The troll was probably right. He smiled. No hard feelings. Frank took a long look at Carl. Scratched his big troll chin.

"You know, not that I mind, but you spend a lot of time with me."

Carl looked at his shoes. "Oh."

"No, really, kid. I don't mind. I like you, even. It's just, I'm wondering...It seems you have friends now. And they're your own species. Don't you think you could talk to them a little more?"

It was something Carl wanted badly. And like other things Carl wanted badly, he wasn't sure how to go about it. He didn't want to scare off Teddy and Bee.

"Well, um. I'm not sure that's how my relationship with them works..."

The troll sighed.

"Sure it is. You just gotta put yourself out there. Ask 'em questions. Give them an opportunity to be heard. You probably do a little of that already. But then open yourself up. You'd be surprised how interesting honesty can be. It's not rocket science, kid."

Carl nodded. It seemed fair.

"Got it. Well, um, we're friends, right?"

Frank sighed. "Technically you're the closest friend I have left in the world."

"So." Carl paused. If they were friends, maybe Frank could finally answer his question. "Why'd you stop defending bridges?"

"Easy, kid."

"Come on."

"Told you, I'm not worthy anymore."

Carl searched the troll's eyes. The troll stared back. Gave away nothing.

"Did something happen?"

"Something I want to keep behind me."

"It, um, can't be that bad."

The troll shook his head. "Let it go."

The boy began to feel uneasy. But his curiosity grew.

"I thought friends were supposed to, uh, ask and tell each other things. What happened?"

"You gotta respect boundaries, too, kid."

Carl rocked on the balls of his feet and crossed his arms.

"Why won't you tell me? It's not like you, uh, made a bridge collapse, right?"

And with a growl, Frank got up and walked toward the scattered rocks. Started tossing them into a pile. Carl felt a knot form in his stomach.

"That's, um, not what happened, though, right?"

"Maybe we should take a break, kid."

"Why? Was it—"

Frank growled again and worked on the rocks.

"Frank?"

Carl watched, worried that he'd pushed too hard. Worried that he didn't know the troll as well as he thought. Worried that maybe Teddy was right to be suspicious. Carl waited for Frank to tell him that it wasn't a big deal, that he shouldn't give it a second thought—anything to ease his concerns. But the troll said nothing. So the boy stood and watched as Frank covered himself in the pile. After the troll finished, Carl watched and waited a little longer—alone.

Then he walked home.

On the way, he attempted to unravel the mixed signals he'd received from Frank. Trolls can be complicated, he thought. Back in his bedroom, Carl watched the rickety ceiling fan spin until his eyelids got heavy. Then he made the questionable decision of putting the glob of troll belly button lint into a ceramic bowl and under his bed. But in fairness to Carl, belly button lint didn't seem like the kind of thing that needed to be refrigerated.

CHAPTER NINETEEN

B ee's bedroom walls were plastered with posters of her favorite rock bands. Bands her mother had listened to as a kid and more recent groups she had discovered on her own. But the posters were the second thing people noticed when entering Bee's room. The first was her art.

Drawings covered her hardwood floors, adorned every inch of wall not shielded by one of her beloved posters, and somehow coated the ceiling, too. Doodles of animals, fantastic creatures, old friends and new. Pictures of Pittsburgh. Comics to remind her of happy days and sad ones. And food—so many drawings of food. Favorite dishes, restaurants, chefs, and servers. Cheery families eating together. Hungry couples being seated by maître d's. There was even a new little sketch of the Chesterfields's truck (though no one was eating there).

Bee brushed her dark hair in front of the little mirror that hung inside her closet door. She frowned at the pink blouse she was wearing. She hated it, but her mother loved it. It felt like a nice gesture to smooth things over and get back on track. And she figured if she "accidentally" got a stain on it at dinner she'd never have to wear it again.

It wasn't that Bee and her mother weren't talking, but they weren't talking as much as usual this week. Bee had given her mother the cold shoulder during dessert at Paris in Spring and on their moped ride home. And for some reason, Bee kept it up for a few days after that. It wasn't like they'd even had a real fight. Bee was simply frustrated with her mother. But then she started to miss their talks. Before long, those feelings outgrew her frustration. Bee couldn't wait for Review Night that evening. Couldn't wait for things to be normal again. That afternoon she even cleaned her room without being asked.

She wondered where they would eat. It had been ages since they'd had Japanese. And she couldn't remember the last time they'd had Ecuadorian cuisine. Or perhaps something low-key could be nice—maybe a tapas place or a Portuguese sausage house?

A knock at the front door shook Bee from her food dreams. She tossed the brush onto her bed, bounded down the hall, and opened the door to find a young woman wearing glasses thicker than her thumb. A massive stack of manila folders was cradled in her arms and reached up to her chin. Bee's face fell.

"You must be Bee," said the young woman behind the glasses and folders.

"Who are you?" asked Bee, but she sort of knew.

"Thanks so much for coming on short notice. Come in, come in!" said Maddy, swooping in from the other room. "Bee, this is Samantha, one of our fabulous interns from the paper." Maddy's face perked up as she noticed Bee's pink blouse. "Don't you look nice."

"I thought we were going out tonight. It's Wednesday."

"Well, yes, but Barry and I—oh, Samantha, look at you with those! Do you want to set them down?"

"Thanks!" Samantha said before spilling the folders across the coffee table and herself onto the couch.

"We always do Review Night together," said Bee.

"I guess we usually do, but Barry and I were—actually, did you want to come with us? I really think it would be good if you got to know him."

Samantha looked up with concern from the couch.

"Oh, don't worry, Samantha. I can still pay you."

The intern's whole face went up.

Bee sighed. "No. I don't need to crash *his* night."

The intern's face went down.

"Are you sure, sweetie?"

"Positive."

"Okay. Maybe we can do something later this week? There

are leftovers from that Welsh restaurant in the back of the fridge. I'm running late. I should go." She pulled Bee to her and kissed the top of her head. "Love that blouse," she said as she slipped out the door.

"Want me to fire up those leftovers?" asked the babysitter, shuffling through the folders.

"I'm not feeling great. I think I'm going to go to sleep early."

Bee slunk away to her bedroom and closed the door. She grabbed a marker from her desk, crouched on the floor, and in the back left corner of her room, between the hardwood and the bottom of her twin bed's box spring, she drew a picture of her mother and Principal Wilkinson eating together in an elegant restaurant. Six inches to the left, she drew a portrait of herself sitting cross-legged, alone. Then she climbed out her bedroom window.

Bee hurried across town to one of her favorite diners and spent two weeks' allowance on a bowl of Cincinnati-style chili (served over spaghetti) and three glasses of lemonade. When she finished, she felt full and frustrated with her current state of affairs. And she felt lonely. She figured it would be hours before her mother got home from her date with the principal.

Then, through the diner's painted glass, Bee spotted the top of a familiar bridge.

Bee watched Mr. Chesterfield's car's taillights pull away as she made her way under the bridge. The food truck was locked up for the night and the rock pile stood tall. If Mr. Chesterfield had had any customers that day, they were long gone.

As Bee approached the stones, she thought back to the afternoon when she and Carl had stared at them together. She still wasn't sure why she'd agreed to go with him that day (boredom, perhaps?), but she was more and more glad that she had. Unlike her mother, Carl seemed like someone she could count on. And for some reason the troll did, too.

Bee leaned into the rocks and whispered, "Frank? Are you in there? It's me. Bee. Lee. Carl's friend?" She felt silly whispering with no one around.

"Hope you don't mind that I came here. I just needed someone to talk to," she said a little more loudly. The rocks said nothing. Bee exhaled and took a seat on one. Tucked her hair behind her ears.

"Have you ever felt unwanted, Frank? Like you've been replaced and forgotten? Do you know what that feels like? To spend your life in a place that's warm and safe and where you're appreciated and loved and then all of a sudden you're an outsider? Like you have a routine? And then suddenly you don't? That's where I am at right now, Frank. It doesn't feel so good. And my mom, the person I'd normally talk to about this kind of stuff, has gone off and found another person to talk to. I know I'm not always the easiest kid to handle, but—I guess I just wish life had a reset button. Or better still, I wish nothing ever changed. Or at least nothing ever changed with my mom."

Bee watched the Ohio River flow.

"We used to do everything together. Going out and talking was always my thing with her, but now it's her thing with him. Tonight she said *I* could go out with *them*. Like he's not crashing our thing? She says I should give him a chance, get to know him better. That I might see he's a 'fascinating, worthwhile person.' Ugh. I mean, he's so old and principal-like."

Bee shook her head.

"Thanks for listening."

"I didn't think we were done talking," mumbled Frank through the rocks.

A smile snuck across Bee's face.

"We're all just looking for our place in the world. I've been where you are, kid. But things might not be as bad as you think."

"How do you know?"

"I don't. But you don't either. Hey, do you think you can get off me so we can do this face to face? That stone you're sitting on is jamming into my ear."

"Oh!" said Bee as she hopped off the rock. "Sorry, I didn't realize."

"See? There's a lot you don't know."

CHAPTER TWENTY

T eddy wore his orange windbreaker every day. Technically it was his big sister Veronica's. After she went off to college his father assured him the windbreaker was unisex. But Teddy didn't care if it was for girls, boys, or unicorns. All he cared about was the fact that it still sort of smelled like his sister, and he liked to be reminded of her while she was far away.

No one at school had ever said anything about his windbreaker before, so he was delighted when Carl boldly slid into the chair next to him during lunch on Friday and asked, "Hey, um, where did you get that jacket?"

Teddy told him all about his sister. And her college. And how much he missed her. It seemed like Carl did his best to chime in with an "uh-huh," or give a supportive nod when he could, but Teddy spoke a mile a minute regardless. He didn't even pause to chew. The boy had a lot to share. It was a special windbreaker indeed.

"And not only is it wind and rain-resistant, it's pretty comfortable, too," Teddy bragged.

"I can only imagine how much wind you're breaking wearing that thing."

The boys looked across the table to see that Bee had taken a seat. She was eating udon noodles from a thermos.

Teddy shook his head. "Very funny, Bee."

"You look like one of those guys on an airport runway who directs traffic with the flashlight things," she said.

"Well, I guess that's another good thing about this windbreaker," said Teddy. "I'll never accidentally get run over by a plane."

Teddy, Bee, and Carl smiled, then turned to their food. As they ate, Teddy tried to remember the last time he'd been so happy and comfortable during lunch—probably never. He glanced around the table and sensed that Carl and Bee were having similar thoughts. He was about to say something about it when the bell rang—it was time to go back to class. Bee popped up from the table, nodded, and headed off.

Teddy figured Carl was about to do the same, but instead Carl asked, "Do you, um, maybe want to come by my dad's food truck after school?"

No one had ever asked to make social plans with Teddy. He wanted to thrust his fists into the air and scream with joy, but instead he surprised himself by playing it cool and saying, "I think I might be able to swing that."

During their walk to the truck, Teddy listened as Carl talked about his family's financial trouble without talking about his family's financial trouble—in a roundabout way. Fumbling through phrases like "The truck is not, um, off to as strong a start as we hoped" and "Things might be a little tight for a while." Teddy could tell Carl was struggling to open up—especially as he mumbled something about "the importance of setting reasonable expectations," but Teddy also saw that Carl was trying his best to share, so he did his best to listen. Which seemed to make them both feel good.

Mr. Chesterfield was over the moon to cook burgers for the boys when they arrived. He'd only served three that day. There would be a massive rush for dinner, he explained. Teddy watched Carl nod along but could tell his friend saw through his father's nonsense. He wondered if Mr. Chesterfield could see through his own nonsense.

Carl and Teddy sat on top of one of the picnic tables to eat their burgers and admire the gorgeous suspension bridge.

"What do you think?" asked Carl.

"Stunning bridge in the daylight," said Teddy. "Definitely one of the city's best. Proud to have the Midnight Brigade watching over it."

"I, um, mean the burger."

"Oh. It's all right. Maybe burgers aren't your dad's strong suit."

"I keep hearing that."

———

Even though the snack from the truck wasn't sitting well in Teddy's stomach, he felt great after talking with Carl. Teddy always had so much to say, but never enough people to say those things to. And despite all they'd discussed, he wasn't nearly done talking for the afternoon.

The first stop on his walk home from the food truck was the craft shop to buy a gift for his father's secretary, Mrs. Bigelsen. Teddy spent twenty minutes explaining to the assistant manager how the new blue yarn they carried had the perfect amount of "hold and give" with knitting needles.

Next, he saw Marvin, the shoeshine guy down the block from his building. Since things were slow, Teddy gave Marvin a shoeshine while telling him all about the scuffed-up pair of loafers he'd seen an old man wearing on his way to school, and how "with just a little care and attention, the loafers could be good as new."

Then he ducked into his building to see Ms. Sanchez, who lived across the hall. They had herbal tea and read the newspaper while Teddy gave a running commentary about an article in the metro section regarding some road repair work. Teddy felt that "anyone driving downtown from East Pittsburgh should plan on adding five to seven minutes to their commute over the next few days, which is the last thing people need when they're just trying to get to work."

When he finally made it home, he dropped his backpack in the middle of the floor, flipped on the TV, and called his sister. He told Veronica all about the hamburger at the food truck, and the blue yarn at the craft store, and the scuffed-up loafers, and the five-to-seven-minute delay for anyone driving downtown from East Pittsburgh over the next few days. Then he asked how her day was going, but by that point she was late for dinner with her roommate and needed to go. So they said their goodbyes and Teddy turned his attention to the television and watched a fascinating documentary about the history of postal codes. Teddy was having an all-time-great day.

Then a local news report interrupted his program. The boy's mouth fell open as he learned that the Hallock Street Suspension Bridge in downtown Pittsburgh had nearly collapsed during a half marathon.

"Something like this was bound to happen," Teddy said to himself with a shake of the head. "Not a single bridge attack since we launched the Brigade? We were due."

The news footage cut to a close-up of some familiar-looking scratches on the bridge and the freckle-faced boy began to steam.

The city was in trouble.

And Teddy Wilkinson was going to do something about it.

CHAPTER TWENTY-ONE

You'll never guess what happened," said Bee as Carl opened the old town house's front door on Friday evening. Carl had a partially eaten, entirely unsold burger from his father's truck in his hand. Bee wore a chocolate-colored sweater. He thought it complemented her eyes. "The Hallock Street Suspension Bridge near Station Square almost collapsed during the Iguana Awareness Club's Half Marathon Fundraiser! The bridge was literally rocking when the first few dozen runners crossed it. The race had to be stopped!"

Carl swallowed the bite he was chewing. "Where'd you hear that?"

"Some guy outside my fifth-favorite El Salvadorian restaurant."

"Should you, um, be talking to strangers?"

"I'm friendly with the valet attendants there," she said with a shrug.

Carl took a moment to process the magnitude of Bee's report. He stepped outside and leaned against the stair railing.

"Wait. Don't you think something like that would've been all over the news?"

"Maybe it is," she said. "I don't really watch the news. Do you?"

"Not really."

Bee grabbed Carl's burger from his hand, took a bite, made a face, and tossed it into the trash can on the other side of the stairs.

"You won't believe what Frank did," declared Teddy as he came marching up the street.

Bee rolled her eyes. "What are you doing here?"

"I came to see Carl," said Teddy.

"Obviously, but did you have to?"

"Yes! Guess what I saw on the news," boasted Teddy, taking two steps at a time to join the others.

"That the, um, Hallock Street Bridge almost collapsed?" asked Carl.

"Well, yeah. Did you watch the news, too?"

"Bee told me."

"Oh."

Carl frowned. "Wait. You, um, think Frank did it?"

"Who else could rock a bridge?"

"No way," said Bee. "He'd never do that."

"I saw scratches on television," said Teddy.

"That doesn't mean it was Frank," said Bee. "Or that the scratches were even related to the shaking."

"He told us bridges moved when he chewed on them," retorted Teddy.

Carl examined his shoes.

"Yeah, but you just said it yourself," said Bee. "When he chewed on them. And only a little. Plus, his tooth is out now."

"Oh, come on. People could have died," said Teddy. "If a troll takes a bite out of a bridge, it's not going to be as sturdy as it was before. He probably has another toothache!"

"Frank wouldn't hurt anyone," said Bee. "Maybe it was the weight from all the runners?"

Teddy shook his head. "That bridge is a hundred tons of steel. And it was *swaying*."

Bee looked at Carl, who seemed lost in thought.

"You're wrong," said Bee. "Tell him, Carl."

Not wanting to pick sides, Carl continued to analyze his footwear. His breathing picked up and his anxiety grew.

"Tell him," she persisted.

Teddy put a hand on Carl's shoulder. "Look, Carl, I understand it's tough to accept, but Frank's the only explanation here. Whether it's something he's doing, did, or will do, it doesn't matter. He's the problem. I don't like it any more than you. I thought maybe we could try to tame him, but that clearly isn't gonna work."

"Tame him?" snapped Bee.

"You know what I mean. We don't really know Frank. Isn't anyone else concerned that he's a troll who gave up protecting bridges? Have you ever heard of such a thing? It's been a red flag since we met him. Who's to say what kind of troubled past he's had in Scandinavia, or wherever."

"Maybe—" Carl stopped himself. Felt his hands sweating.

He wanted to stick up for Frank. But did he know enough to do that? What if he was wrong? Maybe Teddy had a point. Maybe he should tell them about the end of his conversation with the troll earlier that week. Maybe Frank was putting Pittsburgh in danger. Maybe Frank was just a monster living under a bridge.

"Maybe you're not wrong," Carl whispered, surprising his friends. "Maybe we, um, don't really know him."

"Are you serious?" asked Bee.

"You have to accept the facts," insisted Teddy. "A bridge nearly collapsed, and there's only one thing that could've caused that. And he's living next to Carl's dad's food truck. Our city needs our help. We need to tell Frank to get out of Pittsburgh."

"He would never hurt anyone," said Bee.

"There's no other explanation," said Teddy.

Carl looked up from his sneakers. "Why don't we, um, just

ask him about it tonight? We can meet under the awning at twelve-thirty."

"Great," said Teddy.

"Fine," said Bee.

And as the two of them clomped down the steps to go their separate ways, Bee muttered, "Thanks for the support, Carl."

———◆———

Carl stood on the stoop kicking himself. He wished he'd stood up to Teddy. Wished he'd defended Frank. At the same time, he regretted not telling Teddy and Bee about his last conversation with the troll and its prickly conclusion. It was potentially cause for concern, and perhaps Bee would think differently if she knew what happened. Sure, the outcome was the same—they would go to the bridge—but now he was keeping a secret from his friends. And for what? Would Frank even talk to him tonight? Carl had kept his mouth shut and let all his friends down.

Just as he thought things couldn't get worse, he stepped inside to find his mother sitting at her desk in the living room. A letter in her hands. A tear running down her cheek.

"The bank's foreclosing on the house," she said.

Carl's head spun. "What?"

"We're going to lose everything."

Carl stared out his second-story window counting the thirty-three bridges again and again, worrying. When that didn't help, he wrote in his journal. But that didn't help much either.

His family owed more money to the bank than his father had earned the previous year repairing bridges. His mother said they had thirty days to pay everything back. Only thirty days. She said they would need to figure out a plan and all work together. Carl wondered if they should just start packing.

Perhaps if he'd spoken up to his father, he could have talked some sense into him. Perhaps his father would have sold the land and gotten his old job back. Perhaps not. But at least he could have tried. Now they would lose their home. His mother insisted that none of this was Carl's fault, but Carl couldn't help but think that he was at least a little to blame.

The town house was the only home Carl had ever known. He knew every nook and cranny. Knew which doors jammed a little when it rained and which corner of the living room was best for curling up with a good book. He knew which tiles in the downstairs bathroom were a slightly different color of orange and why (and why he would never tell). Which section of the den the swamp cooler hit the hardest on a summer day. He knew what the rug under the coffee table covered, and how far to turn the hot-water knob in the kitchen sink to get the ideal temperature in the guest shower. He knew the sequence of windows to open and close in his parents' room to orchestrate a gentle hum when the wind blew and which floorboards came loose in the attic, creating perfect hiding spots.

Most of all, he knew he could never love a home more than this one.

CHAPTER TWENTY-TWO

The corner with the red awning was one of Teddy's favorite places in the city. He and his father lived in a fifth-floor apartment directly across the street from it. While his older sister had taught him much, one of Teddy's happiest memories was the day his dad taught him to ride a bike around that spot. Teddy loved that awning so much that he snuck out thirty minutes early to wait under it for the rest of the Midnight Brigade.

Unfortunately for Teddy, his father poked his head into his bedroom to check on him twenty-three minutes after he left, as caring fathers often do. Especially fathers who can't sleep after eating at new spicy ramen joints with their food critic companions. Not finding Teddy in bed wasn't what Principal Wilkinson had hoped for. So he checked every inch of the apartment (which didn't take long). After he determined that Teddy wasn't home, he rushed to the nearest window just in time to see Teddy, Bee, and Carl walk off from under the red awning. He was more than frustrated with his son.

Wilkinson put in a quick call to Maddy Lee about her daughter's whereabouts. Maddy told him to sit tight in case the kids came back. She would do some investigating.

———————

As the Midnight Brigade passed the picnic tables, Carl worried they were about to make a horrible mistake. The energy of the group felt off—prickly, even. Bee and Teddy hadn't said much on the walk over. Carl had said less than that.

Even if that bridge had nearly collapsed because of Frank, his toothache was gone now and everyone was fine. What exactly were they even planning to say to the troll? After the uncomfortable ending to his meeting earlier that week, Carl wished they could forget the whole thing. Why not leave the troll in peace and get some sleep so they could try to enjoy City Celebration the next day?

Carl watched Teddy walk with determination. Maybe he should suggest they come back another night, after they had calmed down. But Carl couldn't get his mouth to open. As he wrestled with his thoughts, he caught Bee looking over at him. And it was clear she expected him to do *something*.

He wanted desperately to do anything.

But before he did, Frank poked his head from the bridge's near tower. Saw the serious faces of the children.

"This doesn't look like a social call," sighed the troll.

"Were you at the bridge on Hallock Street?" asked Teddy. Carl gestured for him to take it easy, but Teddy brushed him off.

"Not sure," replied Frank. "I've visited bridges all over this city."

"I know you have," said Teddy in an accusatory tone.

Frank snorted. "For someone who sneaks out of bed all the time, you seem to have strong opinions about what's right and wrong. You're a bit of a contradiction, aren't you?"

Teddy's jaw dropped before he shook his head and returned to the task at hand. "That bridge almost collapsed because of you."

"It did not!" said Bee.

"Yeah, we, um, don't know that," offered Carl.

"What else could it be?" said Teddy.

Frank's face fell. "Did anyone get hurt?"

"Almost. A few dozen marathon runners were crossing it," said Teddy.

"But no," clarified Bee.

The troll took a moment to let the close call sink in. Then looked at the bridge above them and sadly smiled. "This one really is beautiful. One of the best I've ever seen. You don't get into the bridge-defending business to get rich. Sure, the local villagers might bring you a few goats as tribute now and then, but that shouldn't be what drives you. You do it to keep a bridge and everyone you care about on the other side of it safe. I used to protect the most gorgeous bridge in all of Norway. Just flawless. A work of art. But there I was, secretly gnawing on it for years because of my tooth."

The troll cleared his throat. "A perfect bridge made imperfect."

Carl watched tears form in Frank's eyes as he continued.

"My villagers were like my family. I never let a single invader cross that bridge. And my people were tough. Every year they'd go off to raid Sweden. Sometimes they were successful. Sometimes they weren't. But they always came back fewer in number. And it hurt. I never saw the point, going back and forth on who controlled some piece of land or something...but I never asked them to stop. Never said what I wanted. And I missed my chance. Don't ever miss a chance to say what you want, and always be clear about what you mean."

"What happened?" asked Carl.

Frank swallowed hard. "They went off to fight for a whole summer while I chewed on their bridge. And when they marched home victoriously—I'd never seen them so happy—the bridge—the bridge swung and collapsed as they crossed."

"The same thing could have happened to those runners," said Teddy.

"But it didn't," said Bee.

The troll rubbed his soggy eyes. "He's right."

"See," said Teddy.

"I don't deserve to live under a bridge anymore."

Bee's and Carl's sniffles echoed over the Ohio River.

"But your, um, toothache's gone," said Carl.

"Who's to say it won't come back on a tooth that isn't pullable?" asked Frank. "I was good for so long, careful. I even snuck around to different bridges so I wouldn't chew on this one too much. But that didn't matter, and it's beside the point. I knew the risks and did it anyway. I'm an embarrassment to trolls everywhere. I don't deserve to be around bridges anymore. Like I said, not worthy, kid."

Frank hung his head and strolled to the edge of the river. Carl's lips trembled.

"Wait," pleaded Bee.

Teddy crossed his arms.

Frank gazed at Carl. The boy's knees shook as he looked into the troll's eyes. Carl wanted to ask Frank to stay, but he didn't know how to get the words out. And he worried he would say the wrong words. What if Teddy was right? So Carl broke eye contact and stared at the ground.

The troll sighed, turned to the river, and jumped in, vanishing beneath the current.

"Frank!" yelled Bee as Carl's legs gave out and he collapsed. It felt like someone was stepping on his chest.

"It's good that he's gone," said Teddy. "He didn't belong here."

Bee shook her head and brushed away a tear. "You're worse than your dad."

"You don't even know my dad. He's one of the greatest people I've ever met."

"You need to meet more people."

"I don't know what you're even doing here," said Teddy. "I never invited you to join the Brigade in the first place."

"Like I'd want to be in an organization that would have you as a member."

"*Founding* member," corrected Teddy. "Are you going to let her talk to me like that, Carl?"

Carl's heart raced as he looked from Teddy to Bee. The last thing he wanted was to pick sides between friends. So he didn't.

"Whatever," said Teddy as he stomped away from the bridge.

And just like that, the Midnight Brigade was no more.

Carl gasped for air to get the world to stand still. Bee looked down and shook her head.

"Frank's gone because of you. I know you wanted him to stay. And I know you have thoughts and ideas all the time that you don't share. If you keep everything to yourself, you're on no one's team but your own. What are you so afraid of?"

Carl stared up at Bee. "I don't know."

"Be better, Carl."

Suddenly, a flashlight danced between the kids' faces.

"I think it's time to go," said Maddy.

Five things happened before 1:07 a.m.:

1. Teddy walked into his apartment and was grounded for
   the first time in his life. Wilkinson told his son he was
   disappointed in him. The words crushed both of them.

2. Principal Wilkinson vowed to expel Carl from school
   first thing Monday morning. He was furious with the

boy for being such an "awful influence" on his son. Some marching would do him good.

3. Carl was dropped off at his town house. Maddy Lee hadn't wrapped her head around what she'd seen, so she wasn't sure what she would even say to Carl's parents. But when Carl walked through his front door he found his mother waiting for him in her pajamas and bathrobe. She made him a glass of warm milk before sending him tiptoeing to bed. It would be their secret.

4. Maddy and Bee didn't say a word to each other for the rest of the night. They each needed time to think.

5. After the near collapse of the Hallock Street Suspension Bridge and some heated debate, the organizers of City Celebration changed the parade's route. The chairwoman of the committee had been so moved by the love expressed for Pittsburgh in a letter from a young boy that she overruled her colleagues and changed the starting point of the parade based on the boy's suggestion. The announcement coming so last-minute was a logistical nightmare, but better late than never. The parade would begin on Carl's favorite bridge.

CHAPTER TWENTY-THREE

C arl didn't sleep at all that night. He was anxious about Frank. Nervous that it was only a matter of time before one of the bridges the troll had munched on collapsed. Upset that he'd let Bee and Teddy down and caused the Brigade to disband. Worried that things couldn't go back to how they'd been. Carl preferred things the old way. The old way had a place for his family to sleep next month.

It would be hours before the sun came up. So with little to do, Carl checked his email, which shot him from his room faster than he thought possible. Noticing a light on in the living room, he rushed downstairs. He sprang off the bottom step to find his father on the couch. Was his father getting an early start? Had he seen the amazing news? Upon closer inspection, it didn't appear that his dad had showered.

"The parade's starting on our bridge!" exclaimed Carl.

His father shrugged. Barely looked up.

"You should get ready!" continued Carl.

Mr. Chesterfield took a deep breath. Let it out slowly.

"I think it's time to throw in the towel."

Carl couldn't believe what his father was saying. He stared for a moment before taking a cautious seat on the other end of the couch.

"What?"

"It's a failure. I should stop."

"You, um. You can't just quit. Not when family is concerned."

"I can and I should. I actually owe it to you and your mom."

"But I don't mind."

Mr. Chesterfield looked at his son. Scooched closer on the couch.

"But I do, Carl. I tried to make it work, and now I need to try being responsible again. We're going to have to live out of the food truck in a few weeks. The public has spoken. And so has the bank. Not all dreams are supposed to come true."

Mr. Chesterfield's words knocked the wind out of his son, but Carl wasn't ready to give up. "It's just that the, um, parade could be an incredible way to get new customers."

"Possibly. But they won't come back, so tomorrow things will go right back to the way they were."

The boy nodded. "Maybe, um, something could change."

"Am I doing something wrong?"

Carl took a moment to process the man sitting next to him. His father appeared unsure of himself and vulnerable. This was the man who'd showed him how to engineer a perfect pillow fort. Who'd taught him how to pretend to appreciate fly-fishing with his grandfather. Who'd co-built that model rocket they accidentally fired through their neighbor's upstairs window. This was the man who'd helped his mother protect him, feed him, and teach him his entire life.

"It's the burgers, isn't it?" continued Mr. Chesterfield.

Carl swallowed and turned his gaze from his father to the rug under their coffee table. What to say, he wondered. What to say, what to say, what to say? He looked back at his dad and thought about how happy making those burgers made him. How proud he'd been. How defenseless he looked now. It would be so easy to say the burgers were fine. But then he thought of Bee and her advice on food. He remembered his conversations with Frank. Carl loved his father so much. There had to be a better way to respond.

"They're..."

What would his father want to hear? What would be the right thing to tell him?

"They're, um..."

His father looked at him hopefully. Carl took a deep breath, held it.

"They're just not very good."

Mr. Chesterfield flinched. His mouth open, his eyes off his son and on the floor.

Regret washed over Carl like high tide over a beach blanket. He wished more than anything he could turn back time seven and a half seconds, to go back to before his dad had water in his eyes. How could he have been so foolish? So careless about his father's feelings? Why couldn't he have kept his mouth shut like every other day? Maybe it wasn't too late to reel his words back? "Wait! I, um, didn't mean—"

Mr. Chesterfield held up a hand and nodded.

Then he laughed and laughed and pulled Carl in for a hug.

And Carl was overcome with relief.

"Apparently average food for average folks just wasn't as good an idea as I thought, kiddo."

"Well, that's just it," said Carl, smiling. "You can't do the average version of something. All my life, you've been anything but average. You're my dad."

Mr. Chesterfield beamed and gave his son's arm a squeeze. Carl squeezed back. Then Mr. Chesterfield lifted Carl's cap and ruffled his hair.

"We still have six hours before the parade starts," said Carl. "Maybe dreams are easier to achieve when you build them together. We should give it one more shot."

"One more shot," repeated Mr. Chesterfield, nodding to himself. "But we'll need better burgers."

"I think we need something other than burgers," said Carl. "Something that will, um, set your truck apart. Something great."

"Right. But what can we make that's great?"

Mr. Chesterfield and Carl looked at each other and then back toward their kitchen. Perhaps a solution would reveal itself. That was Mr. Chesterfield's favorite kind of solution (Carl's, too). Since neither of them was a remotely talented cook, and because they had little understanding of how most things were made, looking at simple ingredients didn't seem like the smartest way to jump-start their brainstorming, but the two dug through the cupboards anyway.

Flour, salt, sugar? Lifted from the pantry and placed on the kitchen island. Eggs, butter, milk, and cream? Out of the fridge and into the open. Salt, pepper, saffron, and oregano? Taken from the cupboards with a dozen or so other spices they'd only vaguely heard of.

"Maybe rice?" suggested Carl.

"Grab the broccoli, peanut butter, and bacon, too."

By the time Mrs. Chesterfield came downstairs to go to her free early-Saturday-morning tai chi class, the kitchen was a disaster. All the food, ingredients, and cookbooks the family owned were out on display. She was more confused than upset.

But as soon as Carl and Mr. Chesterfield saw Mrs. Chesterfield, they knew what the food truck should be selling.

"Pierogis!"

———◆———

The Chesterfields spent the next few hours making more pierogis than they had eaten in the last dozen years combined. Mrs. Chesterfield led the charge, teaching Mr. Chesterfield and Carl the steps along the way.

They learned to make dough. Then shape the dough into little pockets. Then stuff the pockets with all the wonderful things that Mrs. Chesterfield stuffed her pockets with. Finally, she showed them how to boil the pierogis for just the right amount of time. She thought it best to do the final two steps—the grilling (or adding the love), then topping with butter, sauerkraut, and sour cream—in the food truck after orders were placed so they'd be as fresh as possible for customers.

The Chesterfields loaded the nearly finished pierogis into all the coolers they owned. When they ran out of coolers, they filled Tupperware with pierogis, then put the Tupperware in Mr. Chesterfield's suitcases and packed the luggage with ice.

"We can't afford to go on vacation anytime soon anyway," reasoned Mr. Chesterfield.

Before long, Mr. Chesterfield's little car was filled to the brim. He drove the first batch of pierogis to the food truck's refrigerator and prepped for the day. Carl and his mother would join him after they had cooked enough to fill her car as well. As they finished loading another suitcase, Carl realized he'd nearly forgotten a critical element.

"I, uh, gotta go get something," he said.

Carl hustled upstairs to his room and grabbed the ceramic bowl from under his bed. The belly button lint hadn't lost any of its wonderful smell. If anything, it smelled better after being stored near his dirty socks.

He stared at his bed as one final idea struck. He set the bowl by the doorway, then reached under his mattress and grabbed his journal. He ripped a clean page from the back, sat at his desk, and wrote. His pencil tapped away on the page as the words flew out of him. Then he folded the paper in half, looked out his second-story window, and counted the bridges for good luck. Thirty-two. Thirty-two? Had there always been thirty-two? That didn't seem right.

He counted again and got thirty-three. Odd, he thought as he ran the ceramic bowl and the folded piece of paper out of the room. But definitely not odd in a good way.

As Carl explained to his mother downstairs that he needed to run a quick errand before helping her prepare the next batch, he heard the rickety old ceiling fan in his room finally give out and crash onto his bed with a thump. It didn't feel like the most encouraging sign.

CHAPTER TWENTY-FOUR

F rank sat alone on the bottom of the Ohio River, the current drawing away his stream of tears. Other than to wipe his nose, Frank hadn't moved since submerging himself. As experts know, just like frogs and salamanders (which also often live under bridges), trolls are amphibians. He could sit there for days. Maybe even weeks.

A riverbed was an excellent hiding place for a troll. But other than crying, how would he pass the time? What would he eat? Was cold, wet, and alone any way to live? And how had he gotten himself into this situation in the first place?

Being a troll was challenging during the best of times. Living under a damp bridge and fighting off invading armies, fabled creatures, or the occasional evil sorcerer was no walk in the park. And it was a lonely life. Sure, local townsfolk would say hello or stop to chat as they crossed whatever bridge Frank was protecting, but rarely did anyone make a day of it. And though Frank had been married fifteen times, all his marriages were short-lived. Trolls become much grumpier when they're around their own kind, so two trolls living under one bridge is a recipe for disaster.

But Norway had been wonderful. Not only was the countryside beautiful, but Frank got along with his villagers. They legitimately enjoyed each other's company, and had mutual respect, and their goats were delicious. Frank loved protecting those people and that bridge. He found such pleasure and took such pride in his job. So after his bridge in Norway collapsed, Frank knew he could never forgive himself. He had failed as a troll.

After the incident, Frank wandered Europe. He never allowed himself to become too close or comfortable with any of the townsfolk whose bridges he protected. He kept things professional. And whenever the pain from his tooth became too much to handle, he would simply saunter off into the night. He figured it would be better to leave a bridge unprotected than to be responsible for sabotaging it, but that was no way for a troll to live. So, after a couple hundred years of this behavior, Frank had an honest conversation with himself and decided it was best that he retire.

Frank had long admired Pittsburgh from afar before he decided to make the journey. For decades he had heard the tales about the city with over four hundred bridges. It felt like the ideal place for a troll to spend his golden years. The perfect place to get away from it all and unwind under a bridge. Traveling by night,

he made his way to the Netherlands, and at the Port of Rotterdam he found a ship that would travel across the Atlantic. Then he held his breath, clung to the ship's underside, and hung on.

When he finally arrived in Pittsburgh, the city far exceeded his expectations. The bridges could stand up against any in the world. They were painted stunning yellow or confident black or stood in uncoated steel. It was heaven for a bridge aficionado. Frank had found a place where he could finally be at peace.

But now it appeared it would be best to leave his new life behind. He had given in to temptation and resumed his horribly selfish habit of bridge gnawing—and there were consequences for those actions. But it wasn't only Pittsburgh's bridges he would be running away from.

After Norway, Frank had vowed to avoid making new friends. Then, before he knew it, he was on a path to having three. Three kids he'd brought together. Three kids he'd thought he could inspire. Three kids he should probably never see again.

One of the upsides to the riverbed was that as long as he sat there he wouldn't have to worry about meeting new people. And if he didn't meet anyone, he couldn't let anyone down. He loved Pittsburgh but had to admit that the city might be safer without him.

How much damage had he done to the city's bridges?

What would happen to his friends?

Where would he go?

Why couldn't there be a way for him to fix things?

As Frank pondered and cried, a catfish swam by and smacked him on the nose with its tail.

CHAPTER TWENTY-FIVE

Things weren't sitting right with Bee. And when things didn't sit right with Bee, she did something about them.

On this particular morning, Bee was concerned about Frank. There had to be another explanation for what had caused that bridge with the runners to shake. So the ever-investigating Bee went to the library to wait for it to open. It was there that she made a startling discovery. (Technically two startling discoveries, if you count the late fees she owed on a Korean fusion cookbook she had forgotten to return.)

When she got home, she made a third discovery. On her doormat was a folded piece of lined paper with her name written in pencil. She unfolded the page to find the following:

This Girl I Know

There once was a girl who got me suspended.
It happened while our finances were being upended.

She was strong, daring, fearless, and true.
Someone who always knew just what to do.

But inside she worried she was being forgotten.
Replaced by her principal, which felt rather rotten.

How could someone so singular be displaceable?
A person like her was absolutely irreplaceable.

Did her relationship with her mother need a reexamination?
Or did it come down to a simple miscommunication?

Things might improve if she voiced her concern.
Which is a lesson she wanted me to learn.

Vocal and loyal, she stands by her friends.
Now it's on me to make amends.

She makes me want to be better.
And I'm trying to be.

—Carl Chesterfield

The poem made her smile, then frown, then smile again. She

read it three times before sticking it in her pocket and entering her brownstone.

———————

When Bee returned to her room, her mother was sitting on the bed.

"It was a troll, wasn't it?" asked Maddy.

Bee stood in the doorway.

"You can't be a reporter in this city as long as I have without hearing the rumors," Maddy continued.

Bee took a breath, then a few steps. She sat next to her mother.

"You've been doing some investigating. We're a lot alike, aren't we?" asked Maddy.

Bee nodded.

"Maybe no more investigating after bedtime?" suggested Maddy.

Bee gave another nod. Swallowed. "He's gone now. I'm pretty sure he got blamed for something that wasn't his fault."

Maddy put an arm around her daughter.

"Teddy didn't really give him a chance," Bee continued. "I think you would've liked him if you'd gotten to know him."

"Sounds familiar."

Bee groaned. It was just like her mother to point out something like that at a time like this. "But Wilkinson is my principal..."

"That's only one part of him. He's also a competitive bowler, delightful karaoke singer, terrific father, and mediocre line dancer. And he tells amusing stories that make me smile."

"Is that it? My stories aren't amusing?"

"What do you—honey, you tell the world's best stories."

Bee's eyes wandered the room—a drawing of a flying saucer using a tractor beam to capture a hot-air balloon, the Queen of England playing the tuba with a rock band to the delight of a rambunctious crowd, an elephant riding a tricycle down a grocery store aisle—until she arrived at the portrait of her sitting alone. Her shoulders tightened. She rested her hands on her thighs,

which caused Carl's poem in her pocket to make the tiniest crinkling sound. She took a deep breath. "It's just that things have changed. We don't go out like we used to."

"So that's it. Listen, life is full of big changes and it's up to us to find ways to adapt, okay?"

Bee's heart sank. Then she rolled her shoulders back as she remembered the words of a friend. "No. It's not okay. And I don't want to miss a chance to say what I want, and I want to be clear about what I mean."

Maddy's head snapped back. "Okay..."

"I don't want to 'adapt.' I want things to go back to just being you and me. That's how Review Night should be. I want to spend time with you, not my principal. I miss things the way they were."

Maddy smiled and wrapped an arm around her daughter. "Well, first of all, no one will ever come close to how much I love you. And not everything has to change. I'm going to go out occasionally because I appreciate spending time with this person. And when I do, I really want you to come with us sometimes. You'll have fun. I was serious about that, all right?"

"All right."

"I'm not saying you have to be best friends, but I think you should always give someone a chance before deciding you don't like them. But more importantly, you're right, Review Night will go back to being just you and me. I'm sorry I hurt your feelings, Bee. And between us, he has horrible taste in food."

Bee smiled.

"Also, I'm thinking," Maddy continued, "how about once a week you and I go out to eat wherever you want? As long as it's a place neither of us has been before."

Bee's smile stretched as she eagerly nodded.

"But give him a chance, okay? He's a good one."

Bee took a deep breath. "Okay."

The phone rang in the other room.

"Sorry. Probably work," explained Maddy as she made her way to answer.

Bee's back relaxed as she waited, listening to her mother's muffled voice down the hall. Three minutes later, she heard approaching footsteps before Maddy poked her head into the doorway.

"Well, someone's ears were burning," she said. "Grab a coat, honey. We're getting behind-the-scenes access to the parade. We've got some reporting to do."

"Where are we going?"

"Back to the most interesting bridge in Pittsburgh."

CHAPTER TWENTY-SIX

T eddy slipped away to his father's home office to call his sister
after breakfast. He spun in the swivel chair as he brought
her up to speed on everything—except for the troll.

"And now Dad's disappointed in me, and Carl and Bee
are, too."

"They should be," said Veronica.

Teddy frowned. "I'm not sure I follow."

"They should be disappointed by your actions."

The swivel chair stopped spinning. "Right. That's what I
thought you meant."

"Why'd you sneak out last night?"

"I'm not at liberty to say, but I promise it's for the good of
Pittsburgh."

Veronica sighed. "Got it. Well, you should at least apologize
to Carl and Bee."

"I'm not sure that would be justified. Again, I'll acknowledge
you're at a slight disadvantage by not having all of the informa-

tion, but you're going to have to trust me here. They were kind of out of line, and if anything, they should be apologizing to me."

"What do you want, Teddy?"

"What do you mean? I just want to talk to you."

"No. I mean in life. Do you want to have friends?"

"Of course."

"Then you need to start acting like a friend. Listen to people. Consider other perspectives. Don't be so quick to judge. Or so dead set about being right all the time. If you don't, you're going to be the loneliest kid in western Pennsylvania."

"Oh."

Commandant Livermore was a firm believer in marching. He thought it built character and teamwork while instilling discipline. In his mind, the practice turned children into adults and adults into soldiers—and it turned groups of individuals into units.

At the Pittsburgh Soldierly Institute for Misguided Youths, Livermore had his cadets march everywhere. They marched to class. They marched to the mess hall. They marched to marching practice. They marched to their bunks for bed. Always together, always as a unit. To the Commandant, there was nothing sweeter than the sound of a unit's left feet hitting the pavement, followed by a unit's right feet. Left feet, right feet, left feet, right feet—like a symphony by a master composer.

So when the Pittsburgh (Reserve) National Guard arrived at the far end of the bridge above Carl's father's food truck (which was generally accepted to be on the "outskirts of downtown"), they got into formation and waited for the signal. Commandant Livermore was looking forward to the magnificent sight of twelve hundred soldiers marching from one end of something to the other end of something else, before marching, of course, into downtown Pittsburgh.

If there were any folks who loved City Celebration as much as Carl, it was the Pittsburgh Guard. The group of young soldiers valued their city so highly that they enlisted in the Guard to protect it. And this year they were allowed to proudly lead the parade as their reward.

Commandant Livermore was disappointed to learn that his godson, Teddy, had been grounded. But if a boy got into trouble, witnessing the splendor of professional marching could do him good. So Livermore arranged for his best friend and his godson to be picked up from their apartment and driven to the parade extra early. Teddy and Principal Wilkinson joined him in his jeep, which sat in the middle of the bridge (the car was one of the countless perks of being the deputy adjutant general).

"Pay attention, Teddy. You could learn something today," said Commandant Livermore.

———◆———

Teddy had been lost in thought since his conversation with Veronica. He had spoken fewer than a dozen words over the previous two hours. A personal record. He decided his sister was right, as usual. And because of that, he would need to find a way to apologize to his friends.

Livermore snapped his fingers a few times in front of Teddy's face before the boy processed the twelve hundred soldiers with their twelve hundred rifles getting into formation at the far end of the bridge. A crowd of locals had begun to form at the near end, waiting to cheer on the parade. Teddy frowned.

"This doesn't feel right," Teddy told his godfather.

"Sure it does. The Pittsburgh Guard goes where it pleases. Enjoy the limelight," said Livermore before shouting toward his soldiers. "Ready, troops? Now march together!"

So they did. And the far-off crowd cheered.

Left feet, right feet, left feet, right feet, in rows of twenty over the glorious suspension bridge. The soldiers marched right past Bee and her mother, who were strolling toward Livermore's jeep, Maddy busily taking notes. Principal Wilkinson gave a hearty wave, pleased to see they'd taken him up on his offer. He sprang from the car and jogged in their direction to say hello.

And then the bridge began to purr—which isn't an ideal sound for a bridge to make. Ideally, a bridge would make no sound at all.

"Wait a sec," Bee said to herself as she heard the purr and took in the soldiers marching by.

Left feet, right feet, left feet, right feet, left feet, right feet, left feet, right feet, left feet, right feet, left feet, right feet, left feet, right feet...

Bee scrutinized the soldiers and then, beyond the approaching principal, spotted Teddy in the jeep. Before the purring, Teddy would have been the last person Bee would have wanted to see. But now, after Teddy sheepishly waved hello, they exchanged concerned looks before the concrete beneath their feet shuddered.

Then the bridge began to sway. Just a tad, like a tree rustled by the wind. It leaned a few inches forward, then a few inches back, taking everything on its suspended road with it.

A few inches became a few inches more, then a few more than that.

Teddy's and Bee's mouths fell.

Heads in the crowd cocked to the side.

Commandant Livermore gave an approving nod. Clearly he thought this was some fine marching.

"Well, isn't this nice," said Wilkinson as his jog came to an end next to Maddy and Bee.

Bee was the first to hear the creak. At first it was gentle as a whisper, before building to an unpleasant squeal.

cccrrrrrEEEEEEEEAAAAAAAAAAAAAKKKKKKKKKKKKKKK!

The bridge's road started to rise and fall, like an unsettling wave, as the crowd grew silent. Back and forth, back and forth. Three feet one way and then three feet the other, as though it was made of planks and rope rather than concrete and steel. Soon it wasn't just the ground, but the towers, too. Wave after wave, from one end of the bridge to the other. The structure was playing tug-of-war with itself. The locals watching the parade took several steps back.

Despite the onlookers and all the soldiers, Bee suddenly felt alone. And perhaps a tad scared. A shiver ran down her spine as another purr escaped from the bridge.

Then a familiar set of arms slipped around her and pulled her close. Bee turned her head into her mother's comforting chest, just before she felt her mom shiver. Then Principal Wilkinson wrapped a steady arm around Maddy's back and Bee felt the shivering stop. She watched a frown fade from her mother's face. And for a split second, Bee felt safe, too. Then her mother squeezed her tighter. And she felt loved.

Wilkinson stretched his other arm to grab the bridge. And the soldiers did their best to keep marching. Left feet, right feet, left feet, right feet, left feet, right feet.

Then a moment of clarity hit Bee. "I know what's happening," she murmured.

City Celebration was off to a troubling start.

CHAPTER TWENTY-SEVEN

Mr. Chesterfield felt noble as he loaded the last of the pierogis from his car into the food truck's refrigerator. His soggy luggage wasn't in the best shape, but the pierogis looked wonderful.

The rocks remained scattered around the truck and picnic tables. Carl, Teddy, and Bee would've taken that as a sign that Frank hadn't returned. But Mr. Chesterfield rationalized that the neighborhood kids must be having fun again.

Today would be a fresh start, he told himself.

Today would be an incredible opportunity.

Today the bridge seemed to be rocking in an absolutely unsafe and unintended manner, swaying in a way that steel wasn't meant to sway, causing the City Celebration crowd to move farther and farther away. And boy, there were a *lot* of soldiers marching in that parade.

Mrs. Chesterfield drove with her hands at ten and two. "Are you going to tell me what's in the bowl?"

"Secret ingredient," replied Carl.

"That bowl belonged to your grandmother."

"It, um, washes right out."

"It better, mister."

Carl gasped at the wobbling bridge, approaching through the windshield. "What's happening?"

"That can't be good." Mrs. Chesterfield's mouth hung and her head tilted like she couldn't process what she was seeing. "Hope your father's not just sitting in that food truck. Between us, he can be stubborn."

The car pulled to a stop a few hundred yards from the scattered rocks, safely out of the way of the bridge. Several dozen members of the Pittsburgh Guard who had already navigated the bridge waited around the picnic tables. It seemed they reasoned that the parade's forward progress should pause. Other soldiers did crowd control, cautiously leading any straggling parade-goers a couple of blocks from the sway-ing structure—out of danger and out of sight. The bridge's creak was earsplitting. Its sway unnatural. Seven feet in each direction.

Mrs. Chesterfield honked her horn.

Carl opened his door, popped out, and yelled, "Dad!"

Mr. Chesterfield stood at the near end of the bridge, waving his arms. Futilely trying to get the soldiers to halt. "Stop! Stop!"

Carl's eyes went wide as he spotted his father up on the bridge. He dropped the ceramic bowl on his seat and bolted from the car.

"Carl, wait!" shouted Mrs. Chesterfield.

The sway grew. The bridge was a giant pendulum swinging ten feet in each direction. Carl ran toward his father as fast as he could. The creak grew louder with each step the soldiers took.

"Dad!" Carl called up as he came to a stop below the bridge.

"Carl!" Mr. Chesterfield hollered down.

Bee turned toward the shouting. Her face lit up when she saw Carl at the base of the bridge. "Carl!" She sprinted toward him.

"Bee! What's happening?" yelled Carl.

"It's like Frank's bridge in Norway!" she shouted.

Mr. Chesterfield shrugged, not sure what Bee was referring to but wanting to be helpful. "Or that half marathon!"

"You knew about that?" asked Carl.

"Of course! It was all over the news!"

"Oh!"

Pop!

One of the bridge's cables ripped loose and swung across the bridge, barely missing a row of brave Pittsburgh soldiers. The wavy structure rumbled. Bee watched as Principal Wilkinson pulled her mother away from the swinging cable. Maybe he wasn't such a bad guy to have around. Perhaps she should have listened to her mother sooner and accepted that before they were about to die.

"The lead pack of runners in the half marathon were in lockstep! It was like they were marching!" yelled Mr. Chesterfield.

"So?"

Pop, pop!

Two more cables flew free. Soldiers ducked left and right. Commandant Livermore frowned. He'd seen better parades.

"Suspension bridges can't handle that kind of vibration, Carl!" called Bee. "These soldiers need to break stride! Bridges aren't designed to manage this!"

Mr. Chesterfield nodded at Bee, impressed.

"Seriously?" shouted Carl.

"Seriously!" responded Bee and Mr. Chesterfield.

Pop, pop, pop, pop!

The bridge thundered. Mr. Chesterfield resumed his desperate pleas to the soldiers.

"This swaying doesn't have anything to do with Frank's gnawing!" yelled Bee. "You have to get them to stop, Carl!" Then the bridge lurched and she fell backward, disappearing from sight.

"Bee!" yelled Carl.

He stood and watched the bridge heave back and forth. What could he do? How could he help? As his heartbeat and breathing went into overdrive, Carl registered the frightened faces of the courageous Pittsburgh Guard. It had never occurred to him that a person could be scared and brave at the same time.

Then an idea struck that sent him sprinting toward the Ohio River.

On April 12, 1831, the Broughton Bridge over the River Irwell in England collapsed, injuring twenty people. Nineteen years and four days later, the Basse-Chaîne Bridge in Angers, France, failed, killing over two hundred. Both were suspension bridges. And the casualties were soldiers marching in step across them.

By design, a suspension bridge's cables share the load of a bridge, all working together to lift one small portion of the structure. By design, soldiers march in step to build unity, all working together to project confidence and strength.

When soldiers march in unison (or dozens of marathon participants run in lockstep), their footwork creates a vibration. And that vibration can cause the ground beneath their feet to rise or fall. When the platform of a suspension bridge is raised closer to or dropped farther from its towers, the weight placed on each of the bridge's cables won't be distributed as intended. And when the weight isn't distributed as intended, the structural integrity of the bridge can be compromised, with a cable forced to hold more weight than it was designed to carry. The first sign that a suspension bridge has been structurally compromised would be the bridge's noticeable sway.

For over a hundred and fifty years, soldiers have been ordered to break step when crossing a suspension bridge.

Bee had learned all of this at her favorite branch of the Pittsburgh Public Library. Unfortunately, Commandant Livermore was home sick with the chicken pox the day it was taught in the Pittsburgh (Reserve) National Guard's Officer Candidate School.

———————

Carl came to a halt at the bank of the Ohio River.

"Frank! It's not your fault!" he yelled.

The bridge continued its earsplitting squeal and sway. Cables flew wildly.

"You have to come back! It wasn't you! The bridge in Norway! The runners! None of it was your fault! It was the marching! We need you! Frank!"

Carl searched the rushing water. Nothing.

"I know you want to be here, Frank! This is where you belong— surrounded by bridges! Why else would you pick this city? You wanted to make up for the past, but there's nothing to make up for. You helped me, now come help yourself and all of us! We need you!"

Carl looked up toward the bridge. Steel bolts and chips of concrete sprinkled down around him. He didn't have Frank, but he still had Frank's advice. He had to be bold. So he planted his feet firmly, took a deep breath, and yelled:

"Stop! Stop marching!"

On top of the bridge, Teddy's head jerked back. He recognized that voice (though he wasn't used to hearing that voice projecting). He jumped from Commandant Livermore's jeep, ran to the railing, and looked down to see his friend shouting and waving his arms. "Carl?"

"Teddy! They have to stop! The marching is going to make the bridge collapse!"

Teddy took a moment to process. "Really?"

"Really!"

"Okay! And sorry about being short with you last night." Teddy turned to his godfather. "My friend says they need to stop marching!"

"I didn't realize you had any friends," said Commandant Livermore.

"It's a recent development," explained Teddy. "But he says the marching is going to make the bridge collapse! You have to make them stop!"

"Seriously?"

"Seriously! Please!"

Ordering his troops not to march was a foreign concept to Livermore, but his curiosity was piqued, and he loved his godson. Plus, the bridge seemed less than stable.

"Stop marching!" ordered Commandant Livermore.

And the troops did, baffled to hear that order from their commanding officer. The bridge steadied. The Pittsburgh Guard looked around, confused as to what to do next.

"Now what," mumbled a few.

"You can't march anymore," called Carl from below the bridge. "For now, at least! Just, uh, be, like, individuals!"

The soldiers nodded. It seemed to be a workable approach for the time being.

Bee poked her head over the middle of the bridge.

"You did it, Carl!"

"Bee! I'm glad you're okay!"

"Thanks! Me too!"

"I was worried about you!"

"You were?"

"I was!"

Bee blushed for possibly the first time in her life.

Carl took a deep breath. Not wanting to miss a chance, he looked up and confessed, "Most days you're all I can think about. Those are my favorite days! I want you to know how I feel. Do you think you maybe like me, too?"

Bee did some quick self-reflection.

"Based on how much time we spend together, I'd say the feeling is mutual!"

"Oh! Nice! Did you get my note?"

"I did!"

"Do you think that's part of it?"

"Probably a little!"

"And is this part of it, too?"

"I'd say so!"

"Think we could maybe get something to eat after this?"

"That's really sweet! But it's kind of embarrassing doing this in front of all these people! Could we make plans later?"

"Of course!"

"Bold kid," Commandant Livermore muttered to Teddy.

"That's my friend," Teddy proudly replied.

"That's my son," said Mr. Chesterfield, grinning from the other end of the bridge.

"So, now what?" Commandant Livermore asked Carl.

"Now you should call your people back across the bridge."

"Okay," said Livermore. "Come on back, troops."

The soldiers nodded. The plan made sense. All at once they turned and took a few steps toward the far end of the bridge.

Left, right, left.

Pop-pop-pop-pop-pop-pop-pop!

"Oh no," said Principal Wilkinson as the bridge began to buckle.

"Retreat!" ordered Commandant Livermore.

Maddy Lee, Bee, Principal Wilkinson, Mr. Chesterfield, and several hundred soldiers ran as the bridge sluggishly began to drop.

There's only one thing to do, thought Carl, just before he yelled, *"Frank!"*

Concrete and steel cracked and groaned! Carl felt his stomach turn.

And right on cue, the troll sprang triumphantly from the Ohio River. Ran under the bridge, threw his arms into the air, and held the structure in place.

"Thanks, Frank!"

"Just doing my job, kid," sighed the troll.

The soldiers gasped and gazed in confusion. "What on earth is that?" yelled Commandant Livermore, peering at the troll through a freshly formed crack in the bridge's road.

"Kind of an acquired taste," admitted Teddy.

Commandant Livermore looked down to the few dozen soldiers by the picnic tables.

"Ready, troops!" ordered Livermore.

The soldiers by the tables drew their rifles from their shoulders. Carl's eyes went wide.

"Aim!"

The troll's eyes pinched shut. A few dozen rifles pointed at the creature. Frank's knees twitched and the bridge shook.

"Wait! Wait! He's saving the bridge, you can't shoot him!" screamed Carl.

"He's right!" proclaimed Teddy. "You have to have your soldiers stand down!"

"It's a monster, Teddy!" exclaimed Livermore.

"I don't want to get into another argument over semantics,"

countered Teddy, "but technically he's a troll. And he's defending our bridge!"

"Oh," said Livermore, who loved defending things nearly as much as he loved attacking things. "Lower your weapons. He's defending the bridge."

"Not for long," said Frank, beads of troll sweat running down his forehead. "I can't hold this thing forever. Is anyone here a bridge . . . *repairer*?"

Mr. Chesterfield dug deep into his soul, took a breath, and raised his hand. "I am."

Mrs. Chesterfield smiled at her husband and stood a little taller behind her open car door, proud that he was being of service.

"I'm just gonna need a little help," said Mr. Chesterfield.

"My troops can provide all the assistance you need," boasted Commandant Livermore.

So, as Frank struggled to keep the structure up, Mr. Chesterfield grabbed his tools from his trunk and instructed teams of soldiers on how to help reattach the cables to the bridge. And as each cable was reattached, Frank's load got a little lighter, as the suspension bridge became suspended again.

Forty-seven minutes later the job was finished, and Carl, Teddy, the soldiers, Maddy Lee, Bee, Principal Wilkinson, and

Commandant Livermore applauded the noble efforts of Frank and Mr. Chesterfield. The man and the troll were anything but average.

Then Mrs. Chesterfield encouraged everyone to stick around while her husband fired up his food truck. The parade would have to wait.

CHAPTER TWENTY-EIGHT

Maddy Lee and Bee were handed the first plates of pierogis. Love had been added from the grill. Butter, sauerkraut, and sour cream had been added from the food truck's mini-fridge. And unbeknownst to everyone but Carl, belly button lint had been added from the troll.

Maddy took a long hard look at the food. The last time the Chesterfields had fed her, things hadn't gone swimmingly. But now Mr. Chesterfield was a hero and hundreds of eyes were on her.

She reluctantly took a bite. Her eyes went wide. She took a cautious chew and looked as if she was trying to place the taste. Waited for a moment...then took a *second* bite. A smile spread across her face between chews. Bee winked at Carl.

"My goodness," said Maddy. "These are the best pierogis in the city!"

And the Pittsburgh Guard cheered! Which signaled the City Celebration crowd to finally walk back toward the bridge and make their way down to the truck.

Behind the food truck's window, Mr. Chesterfield threw his arms around his wife and son. Mrs. Chesterfield proudly kissed Carl on the cheek while Mr. Chesterfield lifted Carl's hat and ruffled his hair.

As the soldiers clapped and formed into a line to order, Carl, Bee, and Teddy crept away to look for the giant troll, who had disappeared. They soon found his face sheepishly poking out from the river a few paces from the bank.

"We, um, defended the bridge," said Carl.

"Sort of," said Frank.

"I'm sorry about last night," said Teddy. "You're a good troll. I see that now. And I realize that I said some things I shouldn't have."

Frank sighed. "Apology accepted."

"And I should have stood up for you. I should have said more," said Carl.

"No apology needed, kid."

"I feel pretty great about how I acted," said Bee.

"Well, I always had a pretty great feeling about you."

Frank and the kids smiled.

"I guess I should get out of here while I can," said Frank.

"Where will you go?" asked Teddy.

"Not sure exactly, but I'll be under a bridge."

"Will we see you again?" asked Carl as his eyes grew misty.

"You three? I think it's a safe bet you'll need my help getting out of trouble again at some point."

"Thanks for everything, Frank. You're a good friend," said Bee with a sniffle.

The Brigade and Frank exchanged nods before the troll slipped away into the Ohio River. Carl, Bee, and Teddy dried their eyes and watched the water flow.

As Carl and Bee turned away, Teddy gently grabbed their arms. "Wait a sec. I owe you both a real apology, too."

"You got that right," said Bee.

"That's fair," said Teddy. "Someone might have told me I can be a little . . . judgmental. That I only look at things from my perspective. I'm sorry about that, and I promise I'll try harder. I'm lucky to have you two."

"Agreed," said Carl and Bee, smiling.

The group exchanged handshakes before proudly making their way through the crowd. As Carl rejoined his parents to help in the truck, Mrs. Chesterfield pulled him close and whispered into his ear, "Wonderful things."

By the time Livermore ordered the brave members of the Pittsburgh (Reserve) Guard back into formation to continue the parade, the Chesterfields had sold every last pierogi.

Though the food was gone, hundreds of locals spent the day socializing around the truck's picnic tables and evenly cut grass, appreciating the pleasant atmosphere Mr. Chesterfield had created.

The Guard agreed to break step on all the other bridges they crossed that day, and every day forward. And Carl enjoyed City Celebration with his family and friends more than they'd ever thought possible.

Maddy Lee wrote a glowing review of the food truck for the Sunday paper. She called the Chesterfields' pierogis "transformative." Carl wasn't sure what that word meant when applied to food, but evidently most Pittsburghers did, because the Chesterfields's food truck became the most popular food truck in town. They finally had repeat diners. Customers came back. Two, three, and even four days in a row. Mr. Chesterfield was thrilled.

Maddy wrote an article about Frank, too. But her editor killed the story before it ran.

Apparently the newspaper had a longstanding agreement with the mayors of Pittsburgh not to report on the troll. The thinking being that it might not be great for tourism.

At the request of Principal Wilkinson (though initially from Carl through Teddy), Commandant Livermore's troops were under strict orders not to tell anyone about Frank either. And being good members of the Pittsburgh (Reserve) National Guard, they didn't.

And what happened next? Well, nothing as crazy as how well over twelve hundred people accepted a troll secretly living under a major metropolitan city's bridge.

EPILOGUE

C arl and his father stuck two poles into the freshly cut grass underneath Carl's favorite bridge, then strung a long piece of red butcher paper between them. The homemade banner proclaimed they were CELEBRATING THREE MONTHS OF TRANSFORMATIVE DELICIOUSNESS! in bright yellow paint. Carl thought his father's decision to use yellow on red was more of an eyesore than an eye-catcher, but since they no longer needed to advertise, he shrugged it off.

Like every other morning for the last several months, folks started lining up before the truck opened for the day. As usual, Maddy Lee was close to the front of the line. And that line would grow until the Chesterfields ran out of pierogis that evening. The scattered rocks had been hauled away to make room for eight additional picnic tables. But even with eleven tables, there was always a wait to get a seat.

Teddy, Principal Wilkinson, and Veronica coasted their bicycles to a stop next to one of the picnic tables under the bridge.

"I've received quite a few applications for next year's class of the Brigade," Teddy boasted, his red hair tousled by the late-July breeze. "I'm just not sure when I'm going to find the time to go through them all."

"And what exactly does your club do?" asked Veronica.

"I'm not really at liberty to discuss that," said Teddy.

His sister smirked. "But you need applications?"

"What can I say," said Teddy, "being popular is a responsibility I take seriously."

Carl shook his head as Veronica sighed and hopped off her bike. The Wilkinson family chained their bicycles to the back of the Chesterfields' brand-new food truck. One with a working engine and tires, but one that would remain parked under the bridge that had been saved.

"Great to see you, Carl," Principal Wilkinson said with a wave.

Carl smiled and waved before crouching next to Bee as she applied the finishing touches to her latest masterpiece. Bee had decorated the outside of the new food truck with her art, happily singing to herself as she painted the day away. It was mostly depictions of Pittsburgh's finest bridges, but she had also painted pictures of the Chesterfields, and even included a small portrait of her mother holding hands with the not-so-bad-as-it-turns-out

Principal Wilkinson (though Wilkinson was drawn with her metallic green marker). The centerpiece of the design was a haiku that Carl had helped his father write:

> Don't Be Average
> Be Unexpectedly Great
> All Told, We Are Bold

"I found a great Himalayan restaurant with my mom and Barry this week," said Bee. "Maybe we could go and you could finish telling me about the new bridge they're building in Papua New Guinea."

"Absolutely," said Carl.

Carl looked up through the truck's window as his mother "added the love" to the day's first batch of pierogis. Mrs. Chesterfield liked to help her husband cook on the weekends. During the week she was busier than ever at the dental office—it seemed that the food truck's secret ingredient, while completely safe, contributed to an abnormally high amount of plaque buildup.

Mr. Chesterfield came by and put an arm over his son's shoulder as they admired Bee's work.

"The food truck should probably have a new name," said Mr. Chesterfield.

"Oh, really?" called Mrs. Chesterfield from behind the grill.

"I was thinking Chesterfields & Son."

"How about Carl & Parents?" offered Carl.

"Perfect," replied Mr. and Mrs. Chesterfield.

Mrs. Chesterfield sprinkled lint on a plate of pierogis. "Are you ever going to tell us what this stuff is?" she asked.

"My secret," said Carl.

"I respect that," admitted Mr. Chesterfield. "But no more secrets between your mom and me."

"You got that right," said Mrs. Chesterfield. Carl smiled.

"How about everyone gets in close for a picture?" asked Principal Wilkinson, handing a camera to a gentleman in line.

"Everyone say 'Carl & Parents,'" called Mrs. Chesterfield as she stepped from the truck to join Principal Wilkinson, Veronica, Maddy Lee, Mr. Chesterfield, and the Brigade.

As Carl, Bee, and Teddy wrapped arms and said "Carl & Parents" with the others, the camera went *snap!* and Carl held his friends close.

Whenever the food truck got low on belly button lint, Carl would sneak out to see Frank. Sometimes it would take several nights, weeks, or even a month to find the troll, but when he did, Frank always had plenty of lint. After valiantly defending one of the city's glorious bridges, the troll proudly went back into retirement—though he made it clear he would make himself available if trouble arose. Somehow he always knew to appear when Carl, Bee, or even Teddy needed to vent, or just hear a good tale about protecting a bridge, and he was happiest whenever one of them came to visit. And as one would expect, the Midnight Brigade had many more adventures.

If you ever find yourself in Pittsburgh, be mindful. With over four hundred bridges, there's always a decent chance there could be a grumpy troll nearby. But who knows, he just might become your friend.

Also, try the pierogis. They're delicious.

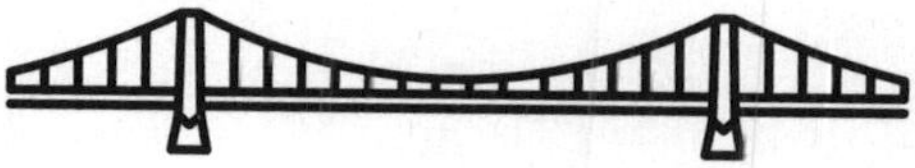

ACKNOWLEDGMENTS

This book was edited by Alexandra Hightower. It's exponentially stronger because of her. A huge thank-you to Megan Tingley and everyone at Little, Brown Books for Young Readers.

Special thanks to Karl Kwasny, Marisa Finkelstein, Barbara Perris, Katharine McAnarney, Marisa Russell, Emilie Polster, Shanese Mullins, Jenny Kimura, Christie Michel, and Mara Brashem.

I am lucky to be represented by Janine Kamouh and James Munro. They helped me shape this story and have been incredible partners and hand-holders. Thanks to them and the wonderful people at WME, especially Alicia Everett, Danny Greenberg, Gwen Beal, Jamie Sweeney, and Laura Bonner.

My parents and brothers have always been recklessly supportive. They should know better. They also all taught me how to tell and appreciate stories.

A big thank-you to my friend Mohsen Nasr, who once told me some interesting things about bridges.

Tons of gratitude to Andy Kimble, Clara Hoffmann, Evie Hoffmann, Kevin O'Connor, Jim Whitaker, Tricia Lawrence, Steve Nuchols, and Adam Levy for early reads and helpful notes.

Thanks to the world's teachers and librarians—mine and yours.

And endless love and appreciation to my best friend, wife, and favorite Pittsburgh yinzer, Erin Malone. She made this book and everything else in my life better.

Erin Borba

ADAM BORBA lives in California with his family. When he's not writing, he helps develop and produce movies for Walt Disney Studios. *The Midnight Brigade* is his first novel.